UNSPARKED

9

A DIFFERENT KIND OF FREEDOM

CORINNA TURNER

unSeen

ALSO BY CORINNA TURNER:

I AM MARGARET series
For older teens and up

Brothers *(A Prequel Novella)**
1: I Am Margaret*
1: Io Sono Margaret (Italian)
2: The Three Most Wanted*
3: Liberation*
4: Bane's Eyes*
5: Margo's Diary*
6: The Siege of Reginald Hill*
7: A Saint in the Family*
'The Underappreciated Virtues of Rusty Old Bicycles' *(Prequel short story) Also found in the anthology:* Secrets: Visible & Invisible*

I Am Margaret: The Play *(Adapted by Fiorella de Maria)*

UNSPARKED series
For tweens and up

Main Series:
1: Please Don't Feed the Dinosaurs
2: A Truly Raptor-ous Welcome
3: PANIC!*
4: Farmgirls Die in Cages*
5: Wild Life
6: A Right Rex Rodeo
7: FEAR
8: A Different Kind of Camouflage
9: A Different Kind of Freedom
10: What's Done is Done†

Prequels:
BREACH!*
A Mom With Blue Feathers†
A Very Jurassic Christmas*
'Liam and the Hunters of Lee'Vi'

FRIENDS IN HIGH PLACES series
For tweens and up

1: The Boy Who Knew (Carlo Acutis)*
2: Old Men Don't Walk to Egypt (Saint Joseph)*
3: Child, Unwanted (Margaret of Castello)*

Do Carpenter's Dream of Wooden Sheep? *(Spin-off, comes between 1 & 2)*

1: El Chico Que Lo Sabia (Spanish)
1: Il Ragazzo Che Sapeva (Italian)

YESTERDAY & TOMORROW series
For adults and mature teens only
Someday: A Novella*
Eines Tages (German)
1: Tomorrow's Dead†

OTHER WORKS

For teens and up
Elfling*
'The Most Expensive Alley Cat in London' (Elfling *prequel short story*)

For tweens and up
Mandy Lamb & The Full Moon*
The Wolf, The Lamb, and The Air Balloon (Mandy Lamb *novella*)

For adults and new adults
Three Last Things *or* The Hounding of Carl Jarrold, Soulless Assassin*
A Changing of the Guard
The Raven & The Yew†

† **Coming Soon**
* **Awarded the Catholic Writers Guild *Seal of Approval***

PRAISE FOR CORINNA TURNER'S BOOKS

LIBERATION: nominated for the *Carnegie Medal Award 2016*
ELFLING: 1st prize, Teen Fiction, *CPA Book Awards 2019*
I AM MARGARET & *BANE'S EYES:* finalists, *CALA Award 2016/2018*
LIBERATION & *THE SIEGE OF REGINALD HILL:* 3rd place, *CPA Book Awards 2016/2019*

Corinna Turner was awarded the **St. Katherine Drexel Award** in **2022.**

PRAISE FOR *ELFLING*

I was instantly drawn in

EOIN COLFER, author of *Artemis Fowl* and former Childrens Laureate of Ireland

PRAISE FOR *A DIFFERENT KIND OF FREEDOM*

This anxiously awaited installment, companion to the previous A Different Kind of Camouflage, *is Josh's survival story in a completely foreign habitat: powerful, suspenseful, surprising, and unexpectedly poignant! First one of this series to bring tears to my eyes! A must read!*

KATY HUTH JONES, author of *Treachery and Truth*

I thoroughly enjoyed A Different Kind of Freedom. *It continues the unSPARKed story, but more that that, it opens a window into the kinds of mental suffering people experience. In this episode, Corinna Turner tackles issues like phobia, depression, and personality disorders in an age-appropriate way that promotes understanding and sympathy. The episode also includes positive examples of seeking help in carrying the burden of mental suffering.*

MARIE C. KEISER, author of *Heaven's Hunter*

PRAISE FOR THE UNSPARKED SERIES

Beware: this series' vivid descriptions, heart-pounding drama, and fabulous characters are sure to lure you in, as well.

LESLEA WAHL, author of the Blindside series

JOSHUA

The fully-grown Dakotaraptor looms over me, lips drawn back from her inch-long teeth. I chirp a cheerful good morning as her distinctive carni'saur scent mingles with the fresh dawn air. She rumbles back in a deeper, more maternal tone, then grabs me by the scruff of my t-shirt. I giggle as she deposits me between her wing-arms, making a half-hearted attempt to fend off the morning preening I know is coming.

Yep, her teeth are running through my hair, getting me spick and span for the day ahead...

I open my eyes. Huh? The stream no longer babbles in my ears. Nostril-searing city-style cleaning products assault my nose. Strange noises and scents. White and brightness hover over me. I blink, turning my head. I don't feel *alarmed*. Just...puzzled.

An unfamiliar room. Small, but with none of the

utilitarian metal cupboards I expect to see. Smooth plastered walls in pale blue. So smooth. No dents, nothing. I'm lying in a bed made of tubular metal. I feel like I've seen it all before, yet it seems so strange...

"Are you awake?"

I blink again, slowly turning my head the other way. A city-man sits beside the bed, dark, dark skin, smart suit.

"Am I?" I murmur. Maybe when I wake from this dream I'll be back beside the riverbank, being groomed by a she-raptor...

"Can you remember your name?"

His voice is so *loud*. I wince. "Joshua Wilson."

"Age?"

"Uh...nineteen."

"Occupation?"

"Hunter." What's the point of all these silly questions? Never mind. It doesn't matter. Nothing matters. I'm sure of that much. I stare at the white ceiling some more.

"Joshua? Are you listening?"

I turn my head again. "*Uh...*"

"I said: do you understand why you're here?"

My wrist—heavily bandaged—is handcuffed to the side of that tubular bed. I stare at the strange sight for a moment. A dim voice, deep inside, suggests this is bad, but I can't feel bothered.

CONTENTS

"Joshua? Why are you here, do you know?"

"Nuh-uh." I shake my head slightly. "I've...no idea." A vague idea of asking this guy floats through my mind, but the white ceiling is swallowing my attention again. So white. Maybe I should...maybe I should find my snow goggles...

"Joshua?" So loud, so rumbly...

"Avalanche," I mutter. I should take cover...except it doesn't matter.

Footsteps squeak away from the bed, then voices, one irate.

"Whatever you're giving him, you *need* to lower the dosage!"

"That's easy for you to say. You don't have to put up with him trying to rip his hand off like an animal escaping a trap—"

"No, *I* just have to defend him in court in three weeks, at this rate without even managing to get his side of the story."

"Just tell them he's psychologically unfit to stand trial."

"The shrinks ruled that he has a severe phobia of the city, but nothing more. Phobias are not on the list of conditions rendering someone unfit to stand trial. After seeing him, I'd question that, but nonetheless. He has to be in that court room in three weeks, so please make sure he's with it when I get here tomorrow, okay?"

"We'll do our best. But you probably won't be getting anything out of him other than screaming and begging and making his wrist bleed."

"We'll see."

The voices go away. I stare up at my snow-scape. Nothing matters.

Or maybe everything is simply fine.

No. *Nothing matters*. Definitely that.

+

The nurse carefully wraps padding around my wrists. She's already done my ankles. She adds extra handcuffs, securing each limb to the bed. I watch her working, unease twisting my stomach. An unfamiliar discomfort. I'm not used to anything *mattering...*

But I'm starting to feel like those cuffs do matter. A lot.

Snick. She fastens the fourth one and looks at me. She's tall, solid, middle-aged, pale-skin, graying blonde hair, and a kind smile. "There we go, Joshua. That should save your wrist from any more damage."

I blink, groping for words. I'm sure I should ask her some stuff, but my head feels packed with feathers.

She grips my arm for a moment, looking at me seriously. "Joshua, the doctor has lowered the sedatives and things she was giving you to keep you calm, okay? They're going to be wearing off over the next hour or so, ready for when your lawyer arrives. Please try to remember what I'm telling you: the extra restraints are just to protect you, okay? You've been pulling too hard on the one wrist. Please try to stay calm. Your lawyer is a nice man, and I think he's going to try hard for you. But you have to talk to him, *calmly*."

I open my mouth and manage a word. "Calmly?" I'm always calm at the moment, ain't I?

"In human words: no, uh, dino-talk, okay?"

I frown. Try an experimental Dakotaraptor croon, hoping I might find myself on that riverbank where I've been spending some of my time.

The nurse smacks my arm lightly. "*No.* Human talk, Joshua Wilson, you hear me?"

I sigh. I'm still here. In...in the *hospital*. The knowledge flits into my head. That's where I am. My gut twists uncomfortably.

I guess she sees the fear in my eyes, because she squeezes my arm gently. "Yeah, you're coming up out of it, aren't you? Just try to stay calm, Joshua. We're on your side."

I think about that as she bustles away. By the time she bustles back in an hour later to give me a drink from the cup I can no longer reach by myself, my gut *aches* with fear and my mind is getting far too clear.

"If you're really on my side, you'd let me go," I mutter.

She tuts and shakes her head. "What use would that

be? Miles of city on every side. They'd catch you again in a twinkling. Anyway, I'm sorry, but you broke the law, taking those kids out into the wilds like that. You have to stand trial. Enough?"

When I nod, she puts the cup back on the bedside table. "Now, your lawyer will be here in about another hour. Try to stay calm until then. Once he's gone, we can dose you up again if it's getting too much."

"No," I say. I hate that state of artificial calm they're keeping me suspended in for day after day. It's like having my mind taken over. Even the fear is preferable to that.

"Well, we'll see how you're doing. Just stay calm really nicely for your lawyer and maybe we can try you on a lower dose."

With that inducement, out she goes.

Just stay calm.

Easier said than done.

Miles of city...

Sweat breaks out all over me.

Stay calm for your lawyer.

That's important. My head's clearing, big-time, and I remember. I remember why that's so important. How well my lawyer does for me will determine how long I'm in-city for, chained to a bed or locked up in prison.

Chained...

Prison...

I swallow, flail my head from side to side as I try to push the thoughts away. *No. No, stay calm, Josh. Stay calm...*

I try to breathe very slowly and deeply, try to concentrate on nothing except that white, white ceiling.

Stay calm.

My heart hammers harder and harder as the drugs wear off.

Miles of city...

Stay calm, Josh.

Prison...

I *need* to stay calm.

Oh, Saint Des, help me!

+

"Joshua Wilson?"

I turn my head as the lawyer approaches the bed. Sweat plasters my hair to my forehead, trickling down my neck, and I'm shaking, but I manage to look back at him and say, "Yes'sir. What d'you need to know?"

"Ah." He smiles. "You're a little more with it?"

"Trying, sir," I whisper.

"Good." He repositions the chair beside the bed and sits. "My name is Phil Gage, and I am your state-appointed defense attorney. I'll try to get through this as quickly as possible. Your case is coming up in three weeks. It's looking likely that the prosecution will only be charging you with felony kidnapping, which is as

7

good as we can hope for. They seem satisfied that no inappropriate behavior occurred and that the farm kids instigated the whole escapade. Now, the most important thing I need to ascertain is that there really is nothing—that is, no evidence of anything more—that could surface to bite us in the behind. Because if they find it between now and then and up the charge to a standard kidnapping charge or add any more unsavory charges, you might be going down for a very long time."

Long time. Long time... I shudder.

"So, Joshua? Is there anything I need to know about?"

I stare at him. "Know about? I thought...I thought you were gonna tell me what you need to know...?"

He sighs. "I just told you, Joshua. Is there anything of...*that nature?*"

"What nature?" He's got me well confused, by now, and it's not just my barely-held-together attention.

He looks at me very closely for a few moments, then nods. "Okay, Joshua, I'm going to ask you some very specific questions, okay?"

"Sure..."

So he does. Half of them make me blush. The other half make me wanna punch him. Have they been asking Darryl this kinda thing? The thought makes my cheeks *ignite.*

He insists that I answer every last one.

+

I sit in the musty courtroom, trying to listen. I'm shaking again, shaking and sweating. Mebbe I shouldn't have spat the pills back out this morning. But I hate the new ones the doc has me on so much. They make me numb inside. Numb and empty. I want to lie down and die.

I tried lying down on the floor at the hospital, once they were letting me up and about, but the nurses just chivvied me to my feet and made me lie on the bed instead. I tried it at the court jail, too, where they transferred me a few days ago, but it didn't work there, either. I just got cold and eventually a couple of other inmates started kicking me.

So I'm still alive, sitting in court with bruised ribs, trying not to lose it 'cos I didn't take my meds.

"Mr. Wilson, are you all right?"

The judge's voice snaps my attention back to the room. Ugh, I've been snaking from side to side, shaking my head as I fight to stay in control. "Fine, sir," I manage. If he thinks I'm unwell he'll insist on a break, and this torture will go on even longer.

Gage eyes me measuringly, so I sit up straight and try to look alert, though I couldn't have told you much about what's been said today. I think some kinda

9

doctor's report was presented earlier, and now the whole atmosphere in the room has changed. People are looking at me less coldly. It's welcome, even if I can't keep track of what's going on.

"Try not to look so wild," says Gage, when we do have a break. "Did you take your pills today?"

I concentrate on drinking my coffee and don't answer.

Don't look wild. Don't look like every city-person's worst stereotype of a hunter, right. How am I gonna do that? But I'm real good at staying still, ain't I?

So I sit for what feels like hours and hours, firmly picturing a T. rex in the middle of the courtroom as I remain motionless, not moving a hair, keeping a calm expression on my face.

I work hard on my T. rex as the hours pass. She's a large female, with pale yellow, almost greenish crest feathers—quite unusual coloring—and hide more greenish than brownish—again, quite distinctive. Her brow ridges are reasonably pronounced for a rex, though nothing like an allosaur's, and the shiny claws on her toes are strong and flawless. She builds a nest as the day progresses and lays four magnificent eggs. I stay stiller than ever. Nothing more dangerous than a proud momma rex...

"Joshua?" Mrs. Rex wavers and vanishes from my

mind as a hand grips my arm.

"What?"

"Are you listening?" It's Gage. "I said, that was the best result we could hope for, wasn't it?"

"What result?" I look around, confused. The courtroom is emptying.

Gage sighs. "They just sentenced you to twelve months in prison with possibility of parole after nine months. You couldn't have done better than that."

I stare at him. "Twelve months?" I whisper. *A year. A whole year* in here?

"Only *nine* months if you behave," he says quickly. "In fact, seven months by now. *Joshua—*"

My control snaps like a thread of cotton in the path of a longneck's leg. I lurch to my feet, bolting toward the nearest door...only to sprawl headlong on the floor as Gage trips me. A second later, the attending policeman is on top of me, pinning me down. I struggle, trying to get free.

"For pity's sake, don't shoot him. He probably needs a sedative..." Gage's voice echoes in my ears as I twist frantically, but I'm still so weak after that infected rex bite and all those weeks chained to a hospital bed. A couple of policemen simply hold me down until I run out of strength and lie, panting and not needing any pills to wish I were dead.

+

I lean against the wall of the prison transport van, too limp with exhaustion to even fight the shackles.

Oh, Saint Des, save me, the shackles. I can't stand 'em. My feet and hands are both cuffed and fastened to a belt around my waist with short lengths of chain. It's even worse than being chained to that hospital bed. You don't expect to be able to run while lying down. But this...

I close my eyes, trembling, and try to pretend they're not there.

Or that I'm not.

+

Prison processing. They make me change my own clothes for a prison uniform, lurid bright orange, the furthest thing imaginable from the khaki and camo I've worn my entire life. I feel like a raw nerve, nakedly exposed. How could I possibly hide, in this?

Guess that's the whole idea.

They trim my hair short, then hand me the few items I'm allowed to keep in a cardboard box. None of it is *mine*; it's just stuff from the hospital. A toothbrush, a couple of physical copies of the Hunter's Journal, a little Bible they said I could take away, though I can't find my favorite stories because it's got some whole books missing...

The guards add some spare clothing, all in that eye-watering orange, and a pile of bedding, then hustle me off toward 'B-wing.' The draft on the back of my naked neck is a chill reminder that I've been shorn.

"Murderers and long sentences are in A-wing," says the younger guard, as we walk. "Medium sentences in B-wing, plus any short-term hunters like you."

The box drags at my bad shoulder, pain spiking. I wanna put it down. I wanna *sit* down.

"See this, kid?" says the older guard, tapping the holster on his hip. "Standard prison-issue taze-gun. They hurt—*a lot*—so don't ever make us use it on you."

"Don't think you can grab it and use it on *us,* either," says the younger guard. "Fingerprint-locked. Only fires for the guard it's issued to. And it has pressure and heat sensors too, so if you wrap your hand around ours and point it at someone, an embarrassing silence is all you'll get—that and a few extra years on your sentence, some of it in solitary."

"Is that all very clear?" asks the older guard.

I mutter, "Yes'sir."

We head on along the maze of concrete and metal corridors in silence, until we reach a particularly robust double-door cage-thing that reminds me of the gate enclosure of an electric fence.

"We don't mix hunters and normal guys unless we absolutely have to," says the older guard as we move through it, "so you'll be sharing a cell with other hunters. You're so young; we'll put you in with the nicer pair."

"Uh...thanks?" I eye the pair of them warily. Are they sincere? Or will they do the opposite, to be mean? I can't tell. My head spins, thick and heavy.

One year.

In here.

I wanna die.

+

We're entering a large hall with three tiers running up each wall, the little galleries lined with sliding doors, currently all standing open. At floor level, rectangular tables with chairs fill most of the space, everything bolted to the floor. Guys in glaring orange sit and mill everywhere. The reek of city-style cleaning products—harsher scents than at the hospital—still fails to overcome a distinct smell of stale sweat along with a hint of even less pleasant things.

The guards take me up to the first level and stop outside one of those sliding doors, each pierced by a little window and a hatch.

"This is you, Wilson. Put your stuff in the empty locker, then go down and mingle. It's tier-time until six, then supper, then back in your cells for the evening at seven."

"Good luck, kid," says the older guard.

They walk away.

I hesitate for a moment, then enter the cell. Empty.

One upper bunk has a bare plasticized mattress—guess that's mine. There's another bunk underneath mine, but the space under the opposite bunk is filled with a desk and three tall metal lockers. A three-man cell.

On one side of the door is a toilet, on the other side, a shower, each with a divider, upper half clear, lower half slightly frosted, to offer a scrap of privacy while not impeding the view from the door much. It smells much better in here than out in the hall, though. A spray bottle standing by the wall in the shower area looks like it probably contains vinda—white vinegar and baking soda—a common natural odor-eliminator used by hunters. Our main goal is to smell of *anything* as little as possible—and above all of nothing tasty.

A narrow window in the far wall between the bunks is the only other thing to see. Basic, cramped, utilitarian metal everywhere—not unlike a Habitat Vehicle. I actually feel more at home here than in that awful hospital.

As far as the surroundings are concerned, anyway. So long as I don't think about...

Don't think about what's outside the walls, Josh. Picture wilderness. Just picture that, and stay calm. 'Cos the wildlife you need to worry about is in here with you.

My back prickles uncomfortably. It's too quiet up here. Quickly, I open the locker doors until I find the empty one, shove my things inside. No locks.

An inexplicable whiff of sawdust teases my nose as I head for the door. A creeping rush of adrenalin is starting to wash my exhaustion away. Supper's soon, is that why everyone's down in the crowded hall? Barely anyone up on these—tiers, are they called?

I'm alone up here, anyway, and this ain't a place to be alone. I need to find a pack, quick as I can.

I only just reach the bottom of the closest bare metal stairway before two older guys approach me. City-guys. One stinks of some highly-scented aftershave product, and they both eye me in a way that makes my back crawl even more.

"Hey, kiddo, you're new. Need someone to show you around?"

His companion shoves his hands in his pockets, thrusting his hips forward, smirking. "Yeah, we're happy to be friends. We'd make real good friends. What d'you say, handsome boy?"

They step closer and I react instinctively, dropping into a hunting crouch and roaring like a very aggressive allosaur warning another allo away from its territory.

They reel back from the full-volume roar, gaping at me.

"*Sheesh.*" The first one turns away. "Ooooookay, the pretty hunter boy is nuts."

"Yeah, maybe not," mutters the other, following his friend, shooting a nervous look over his shoulder.

"Freak probably wants to *eat* us."

Thank God, they keep walking. And are gone. I remain by the base of the stairs, heart hammering. *Everyone* is staring at me. Everyone. *Great*, Josh. Way to make an entrance.

Where's my pack? There are hunters here, the guards just told me so...

Two guys are getting up from a nearby table. Hope sparks inside as they head toward me. 'Cos when you've been scolded for stepping on a twig and praised for avoiding one ever since you were old enough to toddle, you don't clump along like city-folk do. They're hunter-borns.

But are they the 'nicer pair' and how nice *are* the nicer pair, if they're in here?

Yeah, my hope's only peeping out of the undergrowth, cautious as a hunted deer.

They're a lot older than me. The one with the stiffer stride could be in his sixties, lean and boney, with fairly clear-cut Native American features. The other might only be in his fifties, slightly shorter than me and rather angular. Looks like he's mostly white, with mebbe a hint of a few other things. They've both got dark hair. A standard sorta pair of hunter-borns, to the eye.

They stop in front of me, looking me up and down.

"So, cub, are you actually-think-you're-an-allosaur crazy or just crazy-stressed?" demands the older one.

Belatedly, I straighten from my allo-crouch. "Uh, just crazy-stressed, I guess."

"Good. 'Cos I don't fancy sharing my cell with an allo-boy, and that's where you just put your stuff."

Guess these are 'the nicer pair.' Whatever the heck that means.

"I'm Jose Sekakuku and this is Billy Merling," the older guy goes on. Sekakuku. Yep, he's Hopi. "We're co-owners. You can call me Ku."

"Hi, I'm Joshua Wilson."

Billy is eyeing me closely. "Say, are you that cub that can get raptors to do whatever you *misfiring* well want?"

"Uh, I'm real good with raptors, so mebbe so."

He nods, biting at his thumbnail. "Yep, I saw you at a fair, mebbe six years back? Just a real young cub, doing something incredible with a rodeo raptor." He shakes his head. "Ain't never forgotten that."

Sekakuku looks me over with interest. "This is the Raptor Whisperer? What did'ya do to get chucked in here, Joshua?"

"I helped a couple of farm teens stay out-city like they wanted to. City-folks called 'em *children*, said I kidnapped them. But they decided I only did it *technically*, so they say I might be out in" — my voice wobbles but I try to sound positive — "in only nine months. Twelve, tops."

Their gazes, which grew disturbingly intent on me when I mentioned the word 'children,' go more relaxed.

"One year, huh? Lucky cub."

"So, uh, what are you in here for?" I'm not sure about city etiquette, but hunters are allowed to ask this question. We reckon we've a right to know about who we're thrown in with.

Billy bites at his thumb again, while tall, bony Sekakuku shifts his weight—such as it is—from one foot onto the other before answering.

"We had this payment dispute with this city-guy, last spring. He just weren't coughing up. So after a few drinks one night, we figured we'd go and, er, persuade him. Seemed like a good idea at the time. We grabbed him from his house and took him to a bank terminal, and then we found he hadn't paid 'cos he were flat broke. He'd no money to give us. We had to settle for a couple of petty cash cards from his wallet and a rather nice watch and off we went."

"Woke up a few hours later with the cops knocking on our 'Vi door," says Billy glumly. "Five years in here were a terrible trade for a watch and a handful of cash, I tell you."

"Five years?" My eyebrows go up. "When he owed you the money?"

"Armed robbery, they called it," says Sekakuku. "Plus, there was that darn dog of his that tried to eat our faces. Billy settled it, quiet, like, with his knife, but it turned out his kid saw. City-folk really didn't like that."

I don't much like that, and I guess they see it on my face.

"I didn't know that blasted kid were watching," snaps Billy. "Anyway, it were a big dog and it meant business. You gotta do what you gotta do."

I shrug. "I weren't there."

They accept this peace offering with curt nods.

"So, uh, it sounded like there were some other hunters in here?" I kinda hope there are. Hunters have firm rules about mutual protection in prison, but three's a real small pack.

Sekakuku's lip curls. "Sure, there's Sebastian Stevens and Wilhelm Fenn. Another pair of co-owners. City-borns, but they follow hunter-rules, more or less."

"Which are," says Billy, "in case you ain't familiar, cub: mutual protection, no starting fights, no un-necessary mixing, and above all, no getting in with city-gangs."

"I know 'em."

"Good."

"What are they like?"

"Seb and Wilhelm?" replies Sekakuku. "Seb's got a nasty mouth on him at times, though he can be charming when he wants to be. Wilhelm? If you like whipped, muzzled dogs, he's your man."

"I can't stand him," mutters Billy.

Great. Looks like Sekakuku and Billy are probably as good as it gets, as far as company is concerned.

"Come sit down." Billy waves back toward the table they came from. "They'll open up the hatch before long and give us some food." Another wave toward the far end of the hall.

"This the cafeteria, too?"

"Sure is. And that door over there..." He points to the other side of the guard post from the door where I came in. "Opens straight into the exercise yard. They keep us very contained. No need to leave the wing, unless you're on PI or going to chapel or medical."

"PI?"

"Prison Industries. Jobs in the kitchens, laundry, grounds, maintenance, that kinda thing. Very competitive, though. Hunters never get 'em."

"Huh." Not sure I'd want one. Going out might just tempt me to try to escape. And then they'd probably shoot me. Not that a bullet looks unattractive, right now. But I know Saint Des wouldn't want me to seek it...

"Joshua?" They're eyeing me closely.

I straighten and try to push the bleakness from my eyes. "I'm fine."

"First day in here?" Sekakuku rolls his eyes. "*Sure* you are, cub."

"Hunters," Billy says, around a mouthful of iguanodon nugget, "actually do better in here, usually, 'cos we're used to living crammed in small spaces with other guys for long periods. It drives the city-folk wild until they get used to it."

"I ain't gonna find it that easy," I admit, 'cos they deserve fair warning. "I don't do well with being in-city."

"Oh yeah, the Raptor Boy is supposed to be somewhat—" Sekakuku breaks off, then says, "high-strung."

Crazy. Yeah, I never really believed I were *crazy,* but all those weeks freaking out in the hospital and now I ain't so sure. Mebbe I am, after all. But mebbe I can do better, now I'm in a more familiar environment. If I just pretend hard enough that the cell is a HabVi and there's wilderness outside these walls, not city...

Sekakuku tenses, so does Billy. I glance around. A pack of orange has stopped beside our table, a tall, broad-shouldered guy muscling to the front. "I just heard from the guards that this baby-cheeked fish is a *kiddy-knapper.*"

"Yeah?" Sekakuku speaks scornfully. "Since when do kiddy-knappers get twelve month sentences, you greasy gun swab? Did the guard mention that?"

The guy looks unsure, but another guy yells from

the back, "He snatched two kids, yes or no?"

"Guess the court thought no, with that sentence," says Billy.

Everyone starts talking at once. Sekakuku and Billy are tense, but sitting calmly, and I do my best to imitate them. Am I gonna get beat up on day one? The only thing worse than being in prison would be being in prison with my ribs hurting even more than they already do.

Two more tattooed city-guys are approaching. My heart sinks—until they take up a position nearby, quite clearly not with the antagonistic group, and lurk with silent menace. Backing *us* up? These must be the city-borns. Both a bit older than Dad. One is lean, skin either heavily tanned or naturally brown, hard to say which, moderate to light build, almost elegant. Small, watchful eyes, some sorta thorny flower tattooed up the side of his neck.

The other is broad and solid. Not quite built like a bear, but close, his fairly pale skin and blondness are startling combined with the tight Afro curl of his close-clipped hair. What's probably a rex head tattoo peeps onto the back of his hand from under his sleeve, and his knuckles are tattooed as well. Is Almost-Bear Sebastian and Elegant, Wilhelm?

Uncertain of their facts and with five hunters now massed against them, the belligerent group soon bickers on their way, thank Saint Des.

Elegant steps to the end of our table and looks me over. "So, another hunter-born, right?"

I shrug. "Yes."

"*Great.*" His sarcasm ain't flattering.

Almost-Bear comes up to his shoulder, staring at me too. Something protrudes from his mouth—a cardboard lollypop stick? "It's another pair of fists, though, Seb, right?"

Okay, so Almost-Bear is *Wilhelm.* His eyes flick anxiously from me to Seb, waiting for a response.

Seb smirks at me. "I guess he'll do for cannon fodder."

Wilhelm relaxes.

"Get our meals," says Seb, sitting at the table near me.

Wilhelm hurries away. Whipped dog. Right. He returns quickly—no line, by now—balancing two trays. He puts one in front of his co-owner. Seb digs in without thanking him, and Wilhelm sits and starts eating as though he don't notice.

After a while, Wilhelm glances at Seb, clearly checking if he's about to speak, before saying to me, "You wanna swap dessert for nuggets?"

"Huh?" Taken aback, I don't get what he wants immediately. "Oh, you wanna give me your nuggets in return for this apple pie?"

He nods. I'm not hungry. I've barely touched my plate yet, so I almost tell him to just take the pie and keep the nuggets, but barter's probably a big thing in here. When I glance at Sekakuku and Billy, they shake their heads slightly. *Don't do it.* Okay, guess I'd better take my cellmates' advice until I know how things are.

"Uh, sorry, I think I want it." Great. Now I'll have to chomp it down after all. Just the thought makes me nauseous.

Looking glumly unsurprised, Wilhelm starts eating his first course. His dessert bowl is already empty.

I bite half-heartedly into another nugget and chew slowly.

"So, uh, what are you two in for?" I ask Seb at last. I'm already getting the impression he speaks for both of them.

Wilhelm stops eating abruptly, leaving the last nugget on the plate, his face gone tense and wary. His eyes dart to Seb. He makes no move to reply. Muzzled dog, yep.

"Ah, it's a tragic story," says Seb, in the tone of one about to deliver a thrilling yarn. "Lollypop, here, was driving our 'Vi along one night almost a year ago, now, and he ran right into this poor woman's puny little city-car. Mangled it up something fierce. And you know, I *begged* him to stop and help her, but he was in such a panic, he point blank refused. Wanted to head for the border, full-speed, wouldn't listen to reason. Unluckily, we were low on fuel and the cops caught us when we stopped to fill up. It was all very sad. The woman had been eaten by raptors by then, see, but the investigators reckoned that she'd probably survived the actual crash. That she'd likely have lived if"—his eyes dart to Wilhelm, glinting maliciously—"if we'd just stopped to help, the way I wanted to."

Wilhelm stares down at his plate, still and tense as a frightened rabbit. Despite the awful thing he did, I can't help feeling sorry for him.

"People can make terrible mistakes in a panic," I say. "It's a well-known cause of bad decisions."

"All he had to do was listen to me," purrs Seb. "No excuse at all. The voice of reason, of compassion, was right there in his ear. But he chose to ignore it. And now we're in here. Of course, I'll be out in another month and a half, since I was only an accessory. But Lollypop, here, will be in for a long time, yet."

Wilhelm still don't move. You'd think there were a rex in his face, he's so motionless. Seb smirks, like he's enjoying his discomfort, then his beady eyes shift to me.

"So, *are* you in for kiddy-knapping?"

I explain it all again, in more detail—though only saying that Darryl and Harry's Dad appeared to have been eaten by a raptor. Ain't any real chance he's still alive, after all this time, but it's still for them to decide whether to make the kidnapping public knowledge.

By the time I've finished, Wilhelm hasn't broken out of his miserable stillness. Seb still shoots him the occasional glance, a slight smirk on his face as though he's well pleased with the result of his tale-telling.

Heck, these two guys are gonna be fun to be around. Not.

"Wilhelm," I say, feeling real fed-up all of a sudden. "Here, I ain't hungry after all." I slide my apple pie in front of him.

Wilhelm's eyeballs finally move, a startled jerk, followed by a wary glance at Seb. Seb just smirks some more, puts an iggy nugget in his mouth, and starts chewing.

"Thanks," mutters Wilhelm, still looking surprised as Sekakuku rolls his eyes and Billy sighs loudly.

Wilhelm digs the spoon into the bowl and starts single-mindedly shoveling pie into his mouth as though trying to blot out the memory of why he's in here. I force my way through another highly-processed nugget, occupying myself by trying to make out Wilhelm's knuckle-tattoos. Card symbols—heart, spade, clubs, diamond on one hand, with a random star on the thumb. And 'saur road sign warning symbols on the other—rex, raptor, longneck, steg, and a tri.

After a while Seb eats his last bite, wipes his mouth on a napkin and eyes Wilhelm, who's finally looking a little more relaxed as he chews and swallows contentedly. "Seriously, Lollypop, taking some kid's pudding on his first day in here? Only you."

Wilhelm stops eating, glancing from Seb to me with widening eyes. "But he *gave* it to me, Seb..."

"Sure, when you turned on the sad face like that, the way you always do..."

"I *said*, I wasn't hungry," I snap, my temper bubbling up with unusual intensity. "Are you calling me a liar, Sebastian?"

Wilhelm goes motionless again, watching Seb warily, like Seb's the big strong one, not him. Seb eyes me with his nasty little eyes. "Feisty cub, huh?" He glances at Sekakuku and Billy. "Better get a leash on him, pronto, old men."

"You should put a leash on your *tongue*," I retort.

Billy chokes out something that might be a laugh, though he turns it quickly into a cough. But Seb just laughs outright, like he simply finds me funny. Great.

Eventually Wilhelm scrapes up his last bite of apple pie and eats it. Talk turns to our HabVis, Sekakuku and Billy describing theirs to me with Seb making occasional snide remarks, until a voice from a speaker on the wall announces "Five minutes to lock-in" and everyone gets to their feet and heads for the stairs.

Sekakuku grips my arm as soon as Seb and Wilhelm are some way from us in the crush. *"Don't* pick a fight with Seb on your first day. Or any day. No fighting, remember? Least of all among ourselves."

"I weren't gonna *fight* him."

"If he'd gone for you, you'd have had no choice. And he may look like a whippy little piranha'saur, but he fights dirty. A good little cub like you, I bet fighting ain't something you know much about."

He's got that right.

"And why the heck did you give Lollypop your puddin' like that?" grumbles Billy, walking up the stairs behind me. "He's gonna be buzzing around like a wasp, now, hoping for an extra sugar fix."

"I didn't want it. Why waste it?"

"'Cos Wilhelm's a huge pain, that's why," says Sekakuku. "For pity's sake at least take his trade, next time, so he knows it's gonna cost him."

"Sure." I ain't arguing with them. I've gotta be on good terms with my cellmates, or cellies, as they seem to be called. I have to close my eyes and sleep every night in the same room with these guys. We gotta trust each other. "Seb is real mean to him, though."

"Just stay out of it," says Sekakuku. "Ain't none of our business."

"Yep, Lollypop's a big guy," puts in Billy. "He's free to grow a spine any *misfiring* time he chooses."

"Though I ain't holding my breath. Here." Sekakuku steers me into our cell and gives me a push toward my bunk. "Sit on your bed until the guard's been around."

I climb up carefully, trying not to yank on my shoulder or jerk my bruised ribs more than I can help, and settle on the bare mattress. Sekakuku sits down stiffly on the bunk below, and Billy hops more nimbly up to the bunk opposite. They sit, waiting as calmly as though on a stake-out, so I do the same.

From up here, I notice the set of fold-down exercise bars attached to the ceiling, and my heart lifts. This place really is like a HabVi. No reason to let myself turn into a lump of lard. I seriously need to get back into condition. Will I still be seeing the physio? They came to me in the hospital whenever I were lucid enough and had me sit up in bed and do arm exercises. They said if I keep doing them properly, I should have full use of my shoulder and arm back eventually, which is a relief.

Clang.

Clang.

Clang.

Slowly, doors close along the row. Eventually that older guard sticks his head in, his eyes moving between us: one, two, three, check.

"Good night, Hunter One," he says.

"Night, Hurst," Sekakuku and Billy reply, so I say the same.

I see Hurst raise his hand in some signal to the

guard post and our door slides into place with a clang. And locks. *Click.*

"Good night, Hunter Two." The guard's voice comes faintly. Seb and Wilhelm must be next door. I can't hear if they reply, only the clang of the closing door.

And the lock. I've lived my whole life with locks clicking. Locks have always meant safety to me. But here the click sends chills running down my back. Dealing with the human wildlife has been distracting me from where I am, but now sweat breaks out on my forehead. My heart makes an effort to accelerate, but a wave of exhaustion slows it again. The adrenalin is draining away now I'm shut in with only 'the nicer pair' and no one else.

I don't honestly like a single one of the hunters here much, and I don't reckon Dad or Uncle Z woulda made close friends with any of them. But I've socialized around a fire with their type a thousand times. *You can get on with almost anyone,* Dad used to say, *if you're just prepared to make an effort.* I'll be fine, especially with these two cellies of mine. I reckon.

Heck, I'm tired. It's only seven, but I lie down on my side, wincing as my bruised ribs touch the mattress, and close my eyes, desperate for the exhaustion to sweep me into oblivion before I can freak out again.

Tired. So tired...

+

"Why do I have to learn cursive?" Harry groans, as Darryl places the notebook on the 'Vi's table and plunks a pen down on top. "I can already write upper and lower case and type."

"Mom taught me cursive. Isn't that reason enough to want to learn? I know she'd have taught you too!"

I lean across the table, peering at the page as Darryl starts carefully writing out the alphabet. "What is cursive?"

"You know," says Darryl. "Joined-up letters."

"Oh, that fancy historical writing."

"That's right."

"Everything's typed nowadays," Harry grumbles. "It's barely worth knowing normal writing."

"Hey, don't knock normal writing," I say. "I've met city-born hunters who barely can, y'know."

"How'd they get through the city system without learning that? Don't you have to be RTW to get jobs in there?" Read, Type, Write: full literacy.

I shrug. "Guess that's mebbe why some of 'em leave and become hunters." I eye Darryl's pad—she's now adding little arrows all over the place. "Well, you can teach me, if Harry don't wanna learn."

I come awake with a jolt, desperate to pee. Dimness fills the cell, but no true darkness. Light filters in from the outside window and from the little window in the door. The silence of deep night grips the prison—and the cell. Billy's snoring from across the room, below me Sekakuku breathes more softly, but slow and deep. They're both asleep.

When I sit up, my blanket slides off me. One of 'em must've got it out and thrown it over me. They probably are the nicer pair, however hard-nosed.

I ease down from the bunk and pad across to the head, being as quiet as I can and carefully not flushing it. The dull roar of the incinerator in a 'Vi would be loud enough at this time of night, let alone the water that will gush from this city-thing. Once I'm back in bed—and they're still sleeping, good—I pull the blanket over me and close my eyes, hoping to settle off again.

Nope. I'm wide awake, locked in this little cage in the middle of the city.

I shudder, then wince. Darn ribs. Darn shoulder.

The city-light is so intrusive, pushing around my closed eyelids.

No, don't think about the city, Josh.

I sure don't wanna test their niceness by waking them up with a panic attack on the very first night, let alone one of those total crazy fits I were throwing back in the hospital. Mebbe I can avoid any more of those. No handcuffs, here. *Wilderness. Wilderness outside...*

I lie on my back with my eyes tight closed and pretend I'm at home in the 'Vi. Not hard after that dream. Except...*uh-oh...*

Only now, lying here in the not-dark-enough-ness, do I realize how hard I've been trying not to think about a certain thing. Person. *People.*

Darryl's face fills my mind, her brown hair pulled back in her usual braid, her nose freckled from the sun, her blue eyes alive as she drinks in some fresh vista.

Darryl, where are you? Are you okay?

And Harry...his green eyes earnest as he tries to absorb something new, to do a good job, prove he's a man...

My family. My only family, now.

Where are you both? Are you alright?

Longing wraps around my insides and crushes them like a boa constrictor. When will I see them again? Gage said they weren't allowed to see me, that there was no question of it. So not until I'm released? A year, maybe? Unbearable thought.

That has to be borne. Anguish fills me brimful, swells me to bursting. If I were safe, I'd have a good cry right now, no question. But I don't feel safe enough to cry, no way, no how.

I've just gotta lie here and wait for the distractions that morning will bring.

+

The sun is up around five, but it's seven o'clock before a bell rings loudly and the prison fills with the sound of men coughing, talking, showers clicking on,

34

toilets gurgling and sloshing. I guess city-folk don't base their routines on the sun, the way we do.

Sekakuku eases out of bed with a stiffness that says he's getting to the age where he'd be likely to give up active hunting and become a camp-keeper, if he had a camp or camp rights anywhere, which I ain't heard nothing about yet if he does. They strike me as drifters, probably not good with their money. He tosses his blanket up onto Billy's bunk and drags his sheets off.

"My laundry day," he grunts. "Only really time for one lot a day so we'd better do a three-day rotation now you're here."

"Same sheets for three days?" I check. "That's a day too long."

"Smelly sheets ain't gonna get you eaten in here, cub. Three-day rotation."

He plugs the shower drain with a washcloth, tosses the sheets in and chucks some powder on top. Then steps out of his sleep pants and into the shower.

Now I'm puzzled. "Uh...I thought you mentioned a prison laundry?"

"Yeah, they take all the bedding for a proper wash on Fridays."

"*Only* on Fridays?"

"Yep."

Only city-folk would think that washing bedding one single time per week were enough!

Sekakuku is tramping on his sheets as he showers, foaming up the washing powder. Billy goes after him and does the same, though he kicks the washcloth out so the water can start draining away again, rinsing the suds out.

"You're next, cub," says Sekakuku, toweling his short prison fuzz dry. "Just give it a good stomp, then we'll wring it out. It dries by evening."

"Right." I slip off my sleep clothes and step into the shower, but by the time I've had a quick wash they're both standing there, staring.

"Sheesh, kid, what bit you?" Billy peers more closely at the huge scars on my shoulder.

"Massive allo?" guesses Sekakuku.

I shake my head, letting the water stop and grabbing my towel. "Juvenile rex."

"How the heck did you get away?"

"Got an electric prod in the rex's mouth about the same time its teeth pierced my skin. When it felt the volts, it let go real quick, as you can imagine, and before it got a chance to bite down."

Billy whistles. "Lucky cub."

Lucky? I ain't feeling lucky right now. But I guess I am, kinda, just to be standing here at all—even if I'd mebbe rather not be.

"Don't you go telling no one about that," Billy adds, shaking his head, after they've admired my scar a bit more, front and back. "Ain't no one gonna believe it."

"Weren't planning to."

"We wanna hear all about how it happened, though," Sekakuku adds. "But later—we need to wring the sheets."

By the time the bell goes again and the doors slide open, we're all dressed—or as dressed as we can be without a hunting knife between us—and the sheets are hanging from the ceiling. Guess it's time for breakfast.

+

"You Wilson?" The unfamiliar guy in an unfamiliar uniform peers out at me as I reach the serving hatch.

"Yeah?"

"Take these." He holds out a little pot containing two pills, along with a glass of water. Neat lines of the little pots sit in a labeled grid beside him, safely on the other side of the hatch.

Oh. It's a *medical* uniform. Great. My cheeks burning, I take the pot and tip the pills into my mouth, trying to get them under my tongue as discreetly as possible, then take a swig of water and gulp as convincingly as I can.

"Open." The guy has a flashlight in his hand.

"Seriously?" I glance around, humiliated, but no one's paying any attention, other than my cellies. I guess, from all those little pots, I ain't the only guy who needs some kinda pills or other. In fact, something

37

about the way Sekakuku and Billy are waiting makes me wonder if they're expecting to be given something.

"Those are psych pills, so yeah, *open*."

I open my mouth. He shines the flashlight.

"Lift your tongue."

Outage. I shut my mouth, trying to sidle away.

"Nuh-er, Wilson, get back here. Swallow and open, or I'll call up a couple of guards."

"I don't want 'em. They make me feel awful."

"The doctor prescribed them so you have to take them until he unprescribes them. Swallow and open."

I stand, trapped and miserable. I don't wanna swallow those things. The way they make me feel... But being held down and force-fed...

I swallow 'em. Open my mouth again. He takes a good look and waves me on at last.

"Good, Wilson. Go on. Sekakuku, Merling, here you go." He hands two pots to my cellies as I move on.

I get a bowl of reasonably edible-looking oatmeal from the serving hatch and a glass of fruit juice. The server dumps a handful of sugar packets on my tray along with the bowl, without asking if I want them, so I move on without making a fuss.

I've not been sitting down for long when Billy groans—a moment later Wilhelm takes the seat beside me. He eyes my sugar packets but don't speak as he rips open every single one in his own pile and tips them over his cereal.

He sure does have a sweet tooth.

He keeps glancing at my sugar, but he don't say nothing as Seb settles opposite. I nod and give them both a polite "Morning" and get nods in return.

I can't believe they *made* me take those darn pills...

Yep, Wilhelm wants my sugar. He can't stop looking at it. But...huh, he's got a glass of milk. Where he did he get that from? I eye the hatch. Mebbe you have to ask. There's nothing left out, self-service style. Guess that would invite hoarding or food fights. You have to get it all from the servers.

Seb watches Wilhelm, smirking slightly as Wilhelm continues to not open his mouth and offer a trade, though he clearly wants to. I eye Wilhelm's milk. For a full-time 'Vi-dweller, fresh milk is a treat. And it'll coat my stomach, maybe reduce how much of that evil drug I absorb.

I scoop up my packets and hold them out to Wilhelm. "Wanna trade your milk for my sugar?"

From the way his eyes light up, the answer is clear. He slides the glass over to me at once. Soon I'm sipping milk while he's gobbling revoltingly over-sugared cereal. Each to their own.

"And now you're taking the poor boy's sugar as well," purrs Seb.

Managing to control the flash of anger this time, I

ignore Seb, simply raising the milk to Wilhelm in a toast and drinking with relish, a happy smile on my face.

+

I ain't smiling by lunch-time. I don't care about nothing. Sekakuku and Billy walk me down to lunch and sit me at the table, but I push my tray away and rest my head on my folded hands.

"Sheesh, what did they give you this morning?" says Sekakuku uneasily. "'Cos I think I'll stick to my statins, thanks."

I don't answer. Mebbe if I just lie on the table like this for long enough, I'll die.

Eventually my cellies split my sandwich between them, Seb grabs my potato chips and trades them to some city-guy, and Wilhelm the Wasp swipes my apple. I don't care.

They walk me out to the yard after lunch for yard-time, but I curl up on the straggly grass, close my eyes, tight, and carry on trying to die. There's 'soil,' here—the word hunters always use for dirt in formal prayers—and grass counts as 'leaf' at a pinch, so there's everything they need.

But I don't die, because eventually I find myself back in the cell.

+

As soon as the medical guy has finally finished doling out pills this morning and disappeared from

40

behind the hatch, I slip back up to the cell, shove two fingers down my throat and vomit up pills and breakfast together. I'd rather go hungry than be a depressed zombie all day. Sekakuku's and Billy's pills are harmless—nothing but statins and diabetes pills.

I do the same each day, but I can't sleep at night. I keep jerking awake, sweating, feeling like the city's crushing me. I have a full-blown panic attack twice. I try to keep it as quiet as I can, but I wake Sekakuku and Billy. They groan and tell me I'm fine, relax, before going back to sleep. I lie, panting and waiting for dawn—slim comfort though it is.

After four days, I feel like a zombie even without the pills. Head aching, vision blurry, control hanging by a thread.

The wire fence surrounding our exercise yard isn't electrified. It would be easy to climb. I try not to look at it. Beyond is a ten-foot gap, bare sand, then a real old-style prison wall, large blocks of roughly dressed stone. Even easier to climb. I keep my back to it.

There are four guard towers with line of sight to that wall. All with armed guards. And even city-guys can hit a man in bright orange, at that range.

That fence is the one thing I mustn't think about.

Ever.

After yard-time, I move to the window and look out, trying to spot birds above. I keep doing it, can't help myself, but it's a dangerous past-time—the sight of them swooping and soaring, free. Free... Unlike me... The door slides closed. *Clank.* And...

Click.

...something snaps.

I throw myself at the window; I'm screaming, tearing at the bars, hammering at the wall, no words, just frantic, animal noise...

Hands grip me...I struggle wildly...

Voices shout, calling for help...

More hands...*I've gotta get free, I've gotta...*

I'm on the floor, bodies piled on top of me...*I've gotta, gotta get free, I've gotta...*

More running footsteps...a sharp prick in my arm...

Blackness enfolds me.

+

The three city-idiots we rescued from that real mean gang of bachelor pachysaurs have finally finished eating. After roaming around in the ever-mounting blizzard for over forty-eight hours in their little city-car with insufficient...any-thing...they're chilled and hungry and exhausted—and very lucky to be alive.

"Okay," I say, "Bunks. Harry, you can take the fold-out canvas bunk in the cab. Darryl, you have the seat bed. I'll take the footwell. That means two of you guys can take the master bedroom"—I reach up to slap a hand against the sliding door of the compartment over the cab, usually Darryl's private

space—"and the other can have Harry's bunk." I wave up above the kitchen area to what probably looks like just another cupboard to them. They stare blankly.

Harry frowns slightly and opens his mouth, then shuts it again at a level look from Darryl.

Yes, Harry, we could just clear some more cupboard bunks and everyone keep their usual berth, but then we'd have to sleep split up, and it's too soon to be sure what we're dealing with, here.

At least I've got all their rifles secured in our gun cabinet, out of their grasp. In any other circumstances, all my efforts would go toward making sure Darryl had a private berth, but not tonight. Hunters sleep fully clothed anyway and Harry will be there.

Darryl gets it, clearly, because she cuts off any objection from Harry with a cheerful, "Yep, that gives everyone a bed."

Chaos reigns for half an hour as we find spare sleeping bags for them and everyone dodges around taking turns in the shower room and at the kitchen sink, but finally everyone's settled.

Fernando (the Hispanic guy who first ventured out of their crashed vehicle) and Finn, the African American looking guy—who actually turns out to be Fernando's cousin—take the master bedroom. Riley, the other Hispanic guy, takes Harry's berth, whistling to himself in awe at "how tiny this is" as he eases up into it—but hearty snoring almost immediately vibrates out through the thin walls.

Once Darryl and Harry and I are all in the cab, rifles piled in the doorway—and door locked—I crouch beside the dash console, ignoring Harry fumbling the extra bunk out as I turn the speaker volume down low and then access the master bedroom's mikes. It's my Habitat Vehicle, so I have the override codes for the entire system.

Catching on, Darryl crouches beside me to listen as well.

"...can't believe that hunter boy took our rifles," Fernando is grumbling. *"So much for hunters should keep their rifles by them at all times, just in case! What are we supposed to do if a rex shows up?"*

"Wait for Joshua to deal with it with his rex gun, I guess," drawls Finn. *"Our rifles wouldn't be much use against a rex, would they?"*

"You know what I mean!"

"Yeah, yeah, I wish we still had them, but you aren't thinking it through. He's got that pretty girl to think about and the younger boy. He's never met us in his life. He's just being careful."

Silence from Fernando, so clearly he hadn't thought it through. Finally, he bursts out, "He just saved our lives. What does he think we're going to do?"

"We're not going to do anything, except pay him handsomely if he'll take us raptor hunting. But how's he supposed to know that, huh, Nando? There are some real nasty people in the world."

"But we're not!"

"How do they know that? They can't!" Finn's sounding downright irate. "Look, I don't think they're going to rob us. Just go to sleep, cous!"

Irate muttering; rustling of sleeping bags. Gradually silence falls.

Darryl catches my eye. I nod. "Encouraging."

She nods back.

"Fernando's a bit dim, isn't he," says Harry cheerfully, from where he now leans over his sister's shoulder.

"Hopefully decent, more than dim," I say fairly.

"The gun cabinet is out there in the living area, though," Harry points out. "Could they get into it somehow?"

"Unlikely. And even if they did manage to override the locks, we'd hear them."

"You think?" Harry frowns doubtfully.

"I know. That cabinet is bolted directly to the forward bulkhead. Every chink and clang carries straight through into the cab. Dad and I never once managed to get our .22s out for an early morning rabbit hunt without waking Uncle Z, not in years of trying, and that was before I crammed three extra rifles in there. Trust me, if they get anywhere near those guns, we'll know at once. Come on, let's hit the sack."

The ceiling of the prison psych ward is a dingy grey and not nearly so smooth as the hospital ceiling. It's less disorientating to open my eyes to.

I'm very calm. Nothing matters again.

They spend a couple of days easing me off the

tranquilizers, as though that will help, somehow. Of course, once I'm myself again, I'm still in-city, so it's a waste of time.

I beg the doctor to change my pills. The new ones don't keep me so calm, but they don't make me feel quite so bad, neither. After a couple more days, he sends me back to Gen Pop, as they call it. General prison population.

Sekakuku and Billy are both in the cell when I arrive, Sekakuku sitting on his bunk, folding one of his paper boats, Billy at the desk, whittling with his set of highly illicit carving tools improvised from chunks of partially melted and reformed toothbrush handle. They glance around.

"Howdy, cub."

"You alive, then?"

"Apparently." I've been gone a week, but a fading bruise is visible on Sekakuku's cheek and Billy's got a trace of a black eye. "Uh...did I do that?"

They shrug. "We'll live."

Darn. "I'm real sorry."

"Forget it, cub."

"You weren't yourself."

Sure weren't. My knuckles are still scraped, fingernails broken, from scrabbling at that concrete wall.

"Something came for you, cub." Sekakuku nods to

my bunk, where a fat, medium-sized envelope lies.

"For me?" My heart lifts. Could it be from Darryl? By the time I've crossed the cell in two strides and picked it up, my brain's catching up with my heart. It won't be from Darryl. Any indication that I'm communicating with my 'victims' will count against my chances of bail and would probably get them in trouble with that Fernanda woman.

I don't recognize the writing on the outside. It's already been slit neatly open by the prison inspection team. From the expressions of mild interest with which my cellies are watching, I can't tell if they've already satisfied their curiosity and taken a look inside.

I hold it over my bunk and let the contents slide out.

"Huh, an angel singer," says Billy, doing a not-quite-good-enough impression of having never seen it before. "That's nice."

The angel singer is about the size of my outstretched hand, a circle with cord woven across it in an intricate pattern, with a few carved wooden pieces dangling below. A thick bushy fringe of beautiful raptor ruff feathers surrounds the circle—to make angels feel at home. Angel singers are a kinda cross between the noisy wind-chimes city-folks like and the traditional dream catchers still used by Native Americans in the reservation cities, where tribal religions are more common. Native American hunter clans mostly follow

Saint Des—you're hunter first, whatever else second.

The 'silent chimes' on an angel singer are specifically designed *not* to make noise, even hanging at different heights so they can't knock together. Unnecessary noise ain't good in a HabVi. Hunters don't listen to the radio much or watch stuff for hours at a time; you can't do that unless you've someone on watch for anything large enough to be dangerous that gets curious about the racket. Well, some city-borns can't stand the silence of the wilds and they do play their music nonstop or whatever, but they usually pay for it in the end.

Yeah, the fact that we're issued book readers in here but can only view movies a few times a week down in the hall don't bother me at all.

Eagerly, I inspect the circle of the angel singer. The pattern and the items woven into it tell the angels what's on the maker's mind. They can be completely secret and personal, or they can be more obvious, like trail signs or even words. At the top of this one are three lines, and one glance at them tells me it's from West, Thiago, and Ed, no question. The left line is a long black spiral—representing West's Afro hair—the middle, horizontal one evokes a pair of frowning brows— Thiago's got a reputation for being a grumpy worrier— and the right one is a strip of very blond rabbit fur— well, that's Ed.

In the rest of the space are twigs and stones forming the trail signs for 'walk,' 'with,' and 'you.' While they can't actually walk with me, they do in thought. I smile.

"Make sense to you?" asks Sekakuku.

I nod. "Yep." I point to the lines. "My almost-uncles. And I'm sure you can read the rest."

"Ah, *sweet*," mocks Billy.

"Just because you don't get no mail other than your paternity support reminders," murmurs Sekakuku. Billy glares at him.

I just look around for a place to hang the angel singer. The idea is you sing while you make it, and then your guardian angel and any others you can attract, being outside time, can gather to listen as much as they like once it's finished. Like when you leave a candle burning in prayer, even after you've had to go back to your daily work.

I glance at the envelope again. Is that Trudi's writing, mebbe? She and West could be married, by now. And I've missed West's big day. My heart clenches, but I focus on the message in my hand that they've so carefully crafted for me. I'm real glad they haven't put their heads into a noose by coming to see me—but I sure am happy to have this.

+

"Why are the hunters *always* doing laundry?" A young guy hovers in the doorway, peering in, with a

49

slightly older guy next to him. The doors have opened but Billy and I are still twisting my sheets between us, squeezing the water out real good.

"They're hunters; they do what they do." The other guy tugs his sleeve. "Don't stare. You'll make them mad."

He hurries off, but the young guy lingers, still watching us.

Sekakuku eyes him and starts to sing softly, *"Run, rabbit, run, rabbit, run, run, run..."*

Billy joins in menacingly, *"...here comes the hunter with his gun, gun, gun..."*

Getting a scared look, the guy jinks back into the flow of passing inmates and disappears from sight.

Sekakuku and Billy send sinister laughter after him.

"He weren't doing no harm," I object.

"Best to keep 'em afraid, cub," says Sekakuku ruthlessly. "We're seriously outnumbered in here."

"Come on," chivvies Billy, "Let's get this sheet hung up and go to breakfast."

+

Seb and Wilhelm do usually sit at the same table as Sekakuku and Billy—the 'hunter table'—but at a few seats' distance. They keep to that even after I reappear, Wilhelm shooting my cake or sugar only the occasional longing glance. Either Sekakuku and Billy have run 'em off or Seb's decided the mad boy ain't worth his time. I can tell he ain't really forgiven me for talking back to him on day one.

The only time they inch closer is when Sekakuku and Billy talk me into the occasional mimicry display. I stick to quieter animals and 'saurs—no full-out roars to draw attention—but they like to hear me do raptors the best.

Seb—who wouldn't compliment Wilhelm if he walked through fire barefoot to fetch him a cup of coffee—actually shakes his head and whistles as I finish voicing a Dakotaraptor dominance tiff. "If I shut my eyes, I'd believe there was a raptor in here, no question. Sure you ain't part-raptor, Raptor Boy?"

"A hundred percent human," I say, ignoring the subtle insult to my dad. Seb appears to have been commissioned by the devil to test other hunters' self-control.

"See, Wilhelm." Seb's eyes flit to his co-owner. "*That's* how mimicry's meant to be done."

"Why don't you do a velociraptor for us, Seb?" I say sweetly, making Sekakuku kick me in the ankle.

With a sneer and no attempt to mimic anything, Seb withdraws to his usual seat a few places further away.

I dutifully swallow the pills for two weeks, determined to avoid another...incident. But the side effects—so much milder initially—get worse the longer I'm on them until...

I can't breathe anymore. There's no light. No nothing. The prison hall is a great void and I hang here like a fly in a spider's web, and no one would even hear me if I screamed. I have to escape from this, I have to…

But how? Sekakuku and Billy are always there, stuck to me like burrs in a rabbit's fur. They even come to Mass on Sunday, which they ain't never done before. Their grumbling buzzes like white noise in the silence of the chapel, intruding on my fleeting moment of peace.

Lunchtime again. The food sits on my plate, steaming at me. All I can see is the table knife in my hand. So blunt. So, so blunt. But it is pointy…

A weather-beaten, ochre-skinned hand takes the knife from mine, briskly cuts up my meat and withdraws, taking…no…the knife with it. *No…* But I can't protest, can't reach for it… Too hard. I sit, barely seeing my lunch. Until my eyes slowly, slowly follow the steam into the air, up…

And suddenly I feel kinda calm. Because I've seen the way outta this. So obvious. So easy. I've just gotta wait a little longer…

Thud.

My gaze jerks back downwards as Wilhelm knocks the not-well-enough-screwed-down table hard with his knee, making everyone's drinks slosh around. Has he been fidgeting like an antsy kid all meal? Staring at

Seb's apple? Mebbe. I've some dim impression…

Billy slams a hand flat on the table, making everything jolt again as he scowls at Wilhelm. "Quit it, moron! What is your problem today?"

"I've ran out of lollypops and *everything*," Wilhelm says heavily. "And our store-time's not till tomorrow."

Ain't it? I ain't keeping track at all. Cookies and candy, greetings cards, luxury toilet paper, Polaroid film, that's what you can spend your meager allowance on in the prison store, but I don't want nothing. Sekakuku made me buy some candy last time. I think it's still in my pocket, untouched. Is it? Moving a hand to check is too hard to contemplate. What does it matter?

Billy glowers at Wilhelm like he didn't want a reply, let alone one that detailed. Hardly a friendly conversation, but Seb still decides to break it up.

"You keep looking at my apple, Lollypop. You want it?"

Wilhelm's attention snaps from Billy to Seb, his face tightening as he tries to figure out the correct response. My gut clenches and I stare down at my plate, trying to tune them out. 'Cos I've heard enough variations of this conversation by now to know that there ain't no correct response. Seb's gonna get him coming or going.

"Not if you want it, Seb."

"I'm hardly gonna be able to enjoy it, after you've

been looking at it like that, am I?"

"Sure you can."

"You know I won't. Why do you do this to me, Lollypop? You're *so* manipulative. Do you ever think about anyone but yourself?"

Wilhelm hunches lower. Does he understand the way Seb plays him? The cruelty drips into my ears like acid.

I close my eyes tight, pressing my forehead to my fists, but it's no good. I'm drowning. I've gotta escape from all this pain... But I've got a plan. It's gonna be okay. I glance up at the top tier, a good fifty feet above the hard floor of the hall area. I only need a brief head-start. Sekakuku and Billy are old and slow...

When the intercom broadcasts the approaching lock-in, I try to head quickly toward the stairs but my legs don't wanna move, and then Wilhelm's moving along ahead of me—too broad, too slow, his shoulders hunched, steps dragging, walking how I feel. What's it like being locked in with Seb all night and six hours a day? The thought pierces the fog, painful, intrusive...

I slow my stride long enough to gather up the candy from my pocket and shove it into Wilhelm's hand as I ease past him. I ain't gonna need it.

"I saw that," growls Billy. The tiny delay has let him catch up with me. *No, no, no...*

"You sure you're okay, Josh?" Sekakuku's on my

other side, giving me that scrutinizing look of his.

"Fine," I mutter. The top tier calls me. I wanna sprint for it… But they're way too close, now, too alert. I've missed my chance. This time…

I lie on the bed, staring at the ceiling, waiting desperately for the moment when that lock will click open again, let me back out onto those stairs. I can't breathe. *I can't… So dark. So empty. I gotta… I gotta make it stop…*

Saint Des wouldn't like…

Panicking, I shove the faint voice from my mind. No. I can't. I *can't…* I don't dare let that voice in!

Come on, distract yourself, Josh! Do something!

How? Do what? Something. Gotta do something. Magazines? I could…I could get my magazines… My body like lead, I manage to get down from my bunk and plod to my locker, grabbing the handful of magazines I brought from the hospital. That incomplete Bible is on top—my hand brushes it, and I yank away like it's gonna burn me.

I retreat back to my bunk with the magazines. I'm sorting aimlessly through the pile when an envelope slides out.

Joshua Wilson, reads an unfamiliar hand, *c/o Exception State Correctional Department.*

When did I get *this*? Must've been at the hospital. I don't even remember it arriving. The nurses must've simply put it with my things.

I rip it open and a piece of folded paper slides out. On the front is a hand-drawn cross, decorated with flowers, with 'Happy Easter' below it. The sight of the handwriting is like an electric shock, sending prickles and ripples of hot and cold shivering through me.

Darryl!

I unfold the paper at once, my eyes devouring the words.

Josh, I really hope you're okay, or as okay as you can be. I can't say Harry or I like city-life much, but we're well, so please don't worry about us. Maurice may get custody in only two more months. We told the police all about Dad so things will go as easily as possible for you. I'm praying for you every day, and I'm so sorry you're in this mess because of us. Thank you for trying so hard to help us find Dad. I don't know how often I can communicate with you because Fernanda thinks you're evil incarnate, despite the evidence.
Please be well, we miss you so much.
Love, Darryl

Darryl. Oh Darryl...

I read the letter three times.

Please be well, we miss you so much. Love, Darryl

I flop on the bunk, rolling from side to side, twisting in anguish. Heck, I'm *moaning*. But I can't stop. *Indecision and darkness and pain and pain and fear and...*

"*Joshua?*" Sekakuku and Billy loom, peering at me. "Joshua, are you okay?"

Saint Des, help me, what do I do? I had a plan. *Escape...* But I can't. I can't do that to them. Can I? They'll blame themselves. And I know it ain't right, not really... How dare I judge Wilhelm for being spineless, and then...

"Joshua?"

Don't speak, whispers that little voice. *Don't tell anyone. They'll stop you; this will carry on and on...*

But Darry's face is there in my mind; her letter is in my hand...

"No." I force the words from my throat. "I ain't okay. Help me or I'm gonna take a fast-track to hell..."

Two sharp intakes of breath as they recognize the hunter slang, then hands grip me.

"Come on, Josh, let's get you to medical..."

"Come on, cub..."

Though I just managed to ask for help, being held down, restrained...it's too much. I clutch desperately at reason as it slides away from me, but...

+

I'm getting far too familiar with the lumpy grey ceiling of the psych ward. Why am I here again? Right. I totally lost it and got sedated again. It's finally wearing off.

"Can I go back to Gen Pop now?" I ask the prison nurse when she comes to check on me.

She shakes her head. "Doc wants to keep you until he can find something you don't react to so badly."

My heart sinks. I don't wanna be lying here like this, chained to a bed. But those darn pills were gonna kill me.

+

"So, uh, did you think about what I said?" asks Finn in the morning, after the city-guys have each put away enough breakfast for three. "We'd pay you whatever the going rate is for a hunting trip, plus a steep bonus for the extreme weather and the short notice and the trouble."

I sip the last of my coffee and try not to roll my eyes. Outside, the wind still howls, driving loose snow around, a blizzard even without fresh snowfall. I admire his perseverance, but he's clueless.

"We won't be hunting no raptors until this storm dies down. Even if we could get around easy, our prey will be hunkered down in the snow, totally invisible, not moving a muscle."

Fernando waves a hand. "Okay, but when the storm's

58

over. You could fit in a hunting trip before you take us in-city, right?"

"We're not going in-city just yet but our friends are, so they'll be the ones taking you in." Might as well mention that. "Anyway, once the storm's over, we'll be hunting edible meat, the way you guys are chomping through our provisions. You can help with that."

"Herbi'saurs?" Fernando wilts in disappointment.

"Yep, herbi'saurs. And depending on how that goes, then...mebbe...I'll take you raptor hunting."

I ain't gonna say it yet, but we have a culling contract we've been putting off until the weather improves. If they're half-way decent shots they might actually be useful, and we'll get paid extra, which will be welcome, the way the Wilson Vi's income has been for months, now.

Fernando's face lights up, Finn grins. Riley—the most shaken by their near miss yesterday—only musters a weak smile.

I open my eyes as footsteps enter the room, wakefulness arriving in a rush. My heart leaps. "Father Ben!"

He smiles, his teeth gleaming against his dark skin. "Hey, Josh, they let me come see you. How are you doing?"

"I'm chained to a bed in the psych ward of a prison."

He winces. "Yeah, I see that."

"I've been here for..." I trail off. "I don't even know. The days are running together, and I spend half my time like a depressive zombie because of the different pills they're trying me on."

"They said you've been in the ward almost two weeks, this time."

"That long? *Outage.* Yeah, so, not good. Though..." I frown. "I ain't dead yet. Just spend half the time wishing I were. It would probably be better if I were." Guilt surges inside me. "*No, no!* I'm trying not to...to think like that anymore. How are Darryl and Harry, Father Ben? Are they okay?"

Another wince, and a sigh. He sits by the head of the bed and squeezes my arm gently. "Ah, poor Josh. Darryl and Harry are fine. Did you get Darryl's card?"

I nod. "Eventually, yeah. Has their neighbor Maurice gotten custody, yet?"

He shakes his head. "No, and honestly, I doubt he will, and it won't be easy for Darryl to get custody of Harry once she's eighteen, either. But that's a problem for another day. They're safe and well enough for the time being. We need to think about you. How you're coping."

"I'm not. Clearly." No point denying it. I am, after all, chained to a bed.

He grips my hand firmly and I grip back 'cos, though he's Darryl and Harry's friend first and I've only actually met him a handful of times, that kind touch feels *so* good.

"How long have I been here, Father Ben? In prison?"

"It's three months since they caught us."

Three *months*? Huh. A wave of determination grips me.

"I don't wanna let this beat me, Father Ben. I thought I could never survive coming to prison but...if I've survived *three months*, now... I wanna survive the other six or...or nine, if that's how many. But it's so hard! I'm afraid every moment I'm just gonna, just gonna lose my grip for, just for a *second* and something...something bad's gonna happen. *I'm* gonna do something bad, mebbe. That I don't really wanna do."

"Have you been going to Mass?"

"When I were in Gen Pop I did on Sunday. It were real nice, being in the chapel for a while. Made me feel better."

"Then you should speak to the chaplain and get permission to go to daily Mass and Adoration. And see about getting instruction and making your first Holy Communion and getting confirmed, the way we kept talking about you doing as soon as you could."

I stare at him. "I can do all that in here?"

"Of course. All you need is a priest. The prison has

one. Father Timaru. He's nice."

My heart lifts. They even have Adoration here? After getting used to having Our Lord in that little tabernacle in the 'Vi for almost a year, I'm missing His Company. For the first time in weeks, I feel a little surge of...of hope. "Surely that'll help, right?"

He smiles. "I'm quite sure it will *help*. However, don't think it will simply solve everything. It won't change the side effects of any drugs they give you. It won't magic away your phobia or the fact that you're in prison. But, yes, it should help you to *cope* better. Remember this, Josh, because it's very important. You are not alone in here. You are never alone. God is with you all the time. He's in every cell of your body and every cell of the prison. He's in every ray of sun that comes through the window, he's in every molecule of the concrete walls. And Saint Des is right beside you, and your Mother Mary, too."

"Dad?"

"Maybe. If he's done with purgatory. And he can pray for you, either way."

That thought makes me smile.

"I really wanna go back to Gen Pop. I can't stand it in here. If Gen Pop's like a cage, this is like being pinned to a dissection board in a lab."

"Yeah, I get that." He frowns at the handcuff fastening me to the bed. "The doc's got to sort out the pills, though."

"Y'know, they even *make* me talk to those counselor people sometimes, and they go on and on about the city and stuff until of course I lose it, what do they expect? I wish they'd forget the pills and just tranq me whenever I freak out and dump me on my bunk to sleep it off. I'd probably be normal again when I woke up."

He smiles ruefully. "They'll have procedures they have to follow." He hesitates. "I don't know if he'll listen to me, but I will speak to the doc, see if I can persuade him to take you off the pills entirely. Because it sounds like the cure is proving more dangerous than the disease."

"Sure is."

"And if you *do* get down again, speak to the chaplain. Have you tried that?"

I shake my head, unable to meet his eyes. "I were too ashamed. I knew they were real bad thoughts, even though I couldn't seem to stop 'em."

"Oh, Joshua." He sighs, shaking his head. "Something you can't help is not your fault. No need to be ashamed. If it happens again, go to the chaplain as soon as you can, okay?"

"Okay."

"In fact, you tell the chaplain—or someone else, if he's not available—*immediately*. Promise?"

I meet his serious gaze. "Uh...okay. I promise."

He nods firmly. The promise actually eases the tension inside me, slightly. Yeah, a promise means I *have* to tell. That's good.

"Oh, here. Darryl sent this for you." Father Ben draws something from his pocket and holds it out.

My eyes widen, a lump filling my throat.

It's Dad's rosary!

+

"Hey, cub," Sekakuku greets me as I enter the cell, looking up from where he's stretched out on his bunk and smiling.

"Hey."

"Long time no see," says Billy, glancing up from his whittling. He's in his usual seat at the desk, the scent of sawdust filling the air.

"Tell me about it." Out of Psych Ward, finally, after over two weeks. Please let this be the last time! I do feel hopeful, now I've got a plan—a *proper* plan. And Father Ben said he'll try to come see me at least once every month.

"You okay now?" asks Sekakuku.

"Doing better. I don't have to take the pills no more." Father Ben persuaded them, thank Saint Des!

"Good." Sekakuku nods approvingly. "Hard work for a couple'a oldies like us too hafta overpower a strong young cub like you, y'know."

"Sorry."

"Forget it. We found something while you were gone that we thought you might like to have."

"Sure did," says Billy, going to his locker. "Ku caught it."

"What is it?"

He lifts out the largest plastic tub that will fit in the bottom of the locker and hands it to me. Two rough holes have been bored through the lid, no doubt with Billy's sharpened toothbrush tools. A lot of guys keep a sharpened toothbrush tucked away in their cells, with no craft-use in mind, 'just in case.' Fortunately, 'just in case' scenarios happen rather more often in A-wing than B-wing. It's a tamer crowd in here. They've both advised me in no uncertain terms not to sharpen my own toothbrush. With my parole coming up in a matter of months, not years, I mustn't have any misdemeanors on my record—and possessing anything sharp is a big one.

I hold up the tub and take a look. Something small and furry scuttles inside. "Hey, a mouse!"

"Yep. You like it?"

"Yeah!"

+

It's real nice to have something to do, a critter to look after, and it don't take me long to tame Mouse. Soon he's happy to sit in my lap eating cereal or play hide and seek up my sleeve. What with no pills and daily Mass, and knowing Father Ben will be visiting again soon, life's a heck of a lot brighter all of a sudden.

I'm still in-city. But at least I now *wanna* live long enough to get out-city again.

+

Mouse is bored with playing, or mebbe tired. He's curled up in my sleeve and gone to sleep, anyways, so I sit quietly, arm resting in my lap, letting him nap.

Inexorably, my heart drags my mind back to the 'Vi...

"What's the number one rule?" I demand.

"Don't fire until you do," all three city-guys recite at once.

I eye each of them, my gaze lingering on Riley, but he squares his shoulders and gives a firm nod. After three days in the 'Vi and a totally uneventful ornithomimus hunt—to say nothing of the solid hard work of butchering our kills—he's calmed down considerably.

"Good." We're positioned near the area of inaccessible crags in which the pack of Utahraptors makes its home. Though, thanks to the problems they're causing at the nearby ski-resort—harassing the incoming and outgoing buses and monitoring the fence so overtly for any power loss that they're scaring both staff and tourists silly—it won't be their home for much longer. Not if we have anything do with it.

"Culling raptors in winter is actually the easiest time of year to do it," I lecture our hapless rescuees-now-clients.

"Put out some bait and they'll almost-certain come look, unlike at other times of year when they're like to be more cautious. So now we just wait for them to come check out that skinny orni we've got lying out there, tempting 'em."

"It sure is cold." Fernando shivers, trying to tug the collar of his parka up higher. "Can't we shut the windows until they come?"

"Nope. We need to take out the whole pack and there're twelve of 'em. Even with six of us, that means we need to take down six in the first volley if we're to be fairly sure of dropping all the rest once they're alert and running. If any make it back into those crags it'll be a heck of a lot harder to lure 'em out a second time. And if any get away injured, we'll have to go in there after 'em."

Fernando looks excited at the thought of a foot patrol, the fool. Finn looks thoughtful. Riley's lip...quivers. Huh, mebbe he ain't settled down as much as I thought.

"But we won't be doing no foot patrol, will we?" I add bracingly. "'Cos no one's gonna fire until I do, are they?"

"Nope," they chorus.

Darryl rolls her eyes at me. I know what she means. For the three of us to take out all twelve would've required some real fast shooting, but here's hoping our help don't prove more of a hindrance. I'm pretty sure by now that they ain't gonna kill us with a ricochet from not getting their rifle-tip through the bars properly or we wouldn't be doing this for no money. And they can hit a stationary target, so they should *be good for a raptor apiece. That'll have to do.*

"Now it's time to keep quiet and still and wait," I say firmly, 'cos Fernando's still fidgeting with his layers. "I doubt it will be long. You can put up with the cold for a pair of claws, right?"

The thought of his very own claw necklace that's he's a right to—Utahraptor claws, no less—is enough to still Fernando at last.

The sun gleams off what little snow the wind has left on this exposed side of the mountain. The storm was so strong that even in the gullies of the crags most of the snow has been stripped away, and only a light fall has replaced it.

It's not long before the raptors put in an appearance. Darryl tenses beside me as the first head peeps out from a ravine.

"Okay, it's show time," I murmur. "Don't move a muscle yet, but be ready."

Tension fizzes in the air around our three city-idiots but they shift about as little as we could hope. Not enough to be visible through the wide-spaced winter camo-net that's draped over the turret, anyways. Thicker nets cover the rest of the vehicle, along with a dusting of fresh snow.

The matriarch soon lopes across the windswept rock toward the dead orni. Her eyes dart around, head turning warily as she checks for danger but, winter-hungry, she makes swift progress.

"Heck, they're huge!" breathes Fernando, as the rest of

the pack follow her.

"Quiet," I murmur back.

Finn tightens his grip on his rifle. Riley's shaking, darn it.

"The 'Vi is a hundred percent raptor-proof," I add quickly. "We're completely safe."

Riley relaxes a little, but he keeps swallowing jerkily, his eyes fixed to the oncoming predators. With the females standing a head or two higher than a tall man and many times longer, they are impressive. Utahraptors are the very largest raptor species.

"Look at those claws!" breathes Finn. The matriarch sports nine-inch killing claws and even the males have seven-inch ones.

From Riley's gulp, looking at the claws doesn't fill him with the same feelings.

"Quiet," I hiss again, more sharply. "And wait..."

Very, very slowly, I start raising my rifle into position. Darryl and Harry mirror me. Less smoothly, so do the other three.

The matriarch is getting closer. The others are strung out behind her. Two senior pack members are close behind, then three over-eager juveniles. Her mate lurks at the ravine, still, waiting for all the others to pass so he can ride rearguard. We definitely want to get him in the first volley. And that other big female who's attempting to shepherd a couple of more nervous juveniles out of the crags, probably the number two.

The matriarch sniffs at the carcass from a distance, then runs a big circle around it, eyes darting warily. She pauses on the side closest to the 'Vi, sniffing. Such wind as there was blew from the carcass to us when we laid it out, but the fickle aftermath of the storm has already shifted it from us to them. Can she smell our engine, our metal? This pack clearly associate vehicles with possible prey, so it shouldn't scare them off. But it's making her curious.

As she lopes toward us, I check the rest of the pack again. Still too many of them lurking in that ravine. We'll have to wait.

The matriarch's almost to us. I stay motionless. Everyone should copy me. It's clearly impossible to speak or move now without being noticed.

Yep, she's circling the 'Vi. She suspects something's here. Go on, just go eat the orni. Why bother trying to break into a vehicle when there's a meal just lying there?

Makes you wonder how much of the bloody-minded behavior of this pack is entirely down to her, it really does. She jumps onto the hood, thud. *Moving only my eyeballs, I glance at her mate. He's finally leaving the ravine. Soon he'll be far enough away from cover that we can bag him.*

The she-raptor leaps right up onto the roof, sniffing at our camo net.

Riley whimpers…and fires.

Mouse stirs, uncurling from his ball. A flash of resentment stabs me, that he's snatched me back to the present. I'd far rather re-live the mess that city-idiot caused than be here. Longing twists my gut into a painful knot.

Oblivious, Mouse drops from my sleeve into my lap, sits up on his hind legs, and begins to wash his whiskers industriously.

"It ain't your fault, little fella," I murmur, fighting down my pain and disappointment. "So, you wanna play some more when you're done primping, or you wanna go back in your tub?"

+

"But she can see me as soon as she's eighteen, right? Nothing stopping her then!" I try to calm my breathing as I wait for Father Ben's response. 'Cos I must've misunderstood what he just said. I must've!

He sighs so deeply my heart rate kicks up even more. "Joshua, Darryl's only hope of getting custody of Harry is to make the city-folk believe she won't take Harry out-city. So she'll have to avoid all unnecessary contact with country-people. And I'm sorry but, absolutely above all, she'll have to avoid contact with *you*. Or they'll think the two of them are just biding their time before running off with you again."

My chest tightens, like iron bands are crushing it. Darryl's eighteenth birthday in August, that's how long I thought I had to wait to see her. Or at worst, my release, mebbe another three months after, if seeing her would harm my chances of early parole. Not…

"And" — my voice shakes slightly — "how long will it take her to get custody? If she stays clear of everyone…"

A smaller sigh from Father Ben. "That's hard to predict. She'll have to get herself established with an apartment and in a city-job that pays well enough to keep Harry as well as herself. That's not something she can just do overnight. To be honest, she might not realistically be ready to make an attempt for at least a year."

"From now?" An embarrassing squeak to my voice this time.

"From when she's eighteen." Father Ben speaks very gently.

The room, the prison, the entire city zooms in on me, pressing hard, as though a giant fist is crushing it like a ball, with me at the center, a tiny, insignificant, lonely dot. I press my forehead to the heels of my hands, breathing hard, fighting for control.

I was resigned to not being able to see Harry any time soon, not until Darryl had custody again. But Darryl…

"I'm really sorry. I know this is not what you wanted to hear."

"Time's up." The guard appears beside the little visiting table.

"The weeks will go quickly, Josh," adds Father Ben. "Keep praying. Get to Mass. You'll be okay. And I'll be back here next week; I'm in-city again then. Okay?"

I manage a nod, but I walk back to my cell in a daze. I feel so low I go straight to get Mouse out of his tub in the locker, but he's sound asleep, so I leave him alone and read Darryl's letter for the millionth time instead, then rest it on my chest, staring at the bleak concrete ceiling.

Okay. Am I okay? Will I be okay?

I'm so alone.

+

I sit on the bleachers in the yard, arms wrapped around my knees. I wish Sekakuku and Billy would come back, but they've both gone off to trade.

Although they've stopped worrying so much about leaving me by myself, these days, I think Sekakuku thought Billy was gonna be with me when he went off to see about greaseproof paper from the guys who work in the kitchen—for his boats. But Billy's out of wood for his whittling.

I feel bad inside today. Frantic.

Father Ben made me promise...

But I don't feel how the pills made me feel, exactly. I just feel...

I wanna be anywhere but here. So bad. The need grips me like a vice, seethes inside, spins me around and sweeps over me like a flash flood. Not quite my full phobia kicking in, more like some dismal blend of phobia and gloom.

I need to get outta here!

My eyes find the fence, on the side where the wall is. Heck, it's easy to climb. And the wall. So easy. Nothing to it.

They'd see you, Josh. They'd see you and shoot you.

What if they didn't?

In your bright orange kit?

If I made it over? Into the city, looming beyond. Hid under some truck, mebbe, made it out the gates...

I'd be free...

They'll shoot you, Josh.

It's not impossible, right? Someone did escape, years ago.

He was recaptured, Josh.

Only because he didn't know how to disappear into the wilderness and live like Saint Des. I could do it. I ain't gonna be able to see Darryl and Harry for who knows how long. I might as well go and live in the wilds and be happy.

I glance over my shoulder. Sekakuku and Billy are still bargaining hard. The fence sucks my eyes back to it. Mebbe I should go ask to see the chaplain. The doctor, even... I shouldn't be thinking about this. What's the difference between this and how I were thinking before?

A chance. That's the difference. It's okay to seek freedom. And if I end up with the other kind...so be it.

I shake my head from side to side, trying to drive the thoughts away.

The fence. It hooks my gaze again, reeling me in like a fish on a line.

Freedom. If I can just make it over that, I've got a real chance. The wilderness fills my mind. Lush and green, this time of year. Running streams, wildlife... Scents and sounds...

I lick my lips, unable to look away, though it's barely the fence I'm seeing.

Freedom.

Don't do it, Josh.

I've gotta try...

Don't do it, Josh!

I can't, I can't just sit here. I—

My arms unwrap from my knees. My feet drop from the bleacher to the ground. I'm on my feet, muscles tensing—

Don't, Josh...

I start to move—and a pair of arms clamp around me, holding me in place. I recognize the tattoos even before a deep voice says in my ear, "Don't do it, kid."

"Let me go!" I wrench, trying to get free. Heck, why did I ever label him an *almost*-bear? He's a bear, alright.

Real strong.

"Ur...*no.*"

"Get off me, Wilhelm! You're making me mad at you!"

"Mad's better than dead. I'll let you go when you calm down."

"I am calm!"

"Sure, you're about to get yourself plugged full of holes 'cos you're *fine.*"

"I'm trying to *escape,* you stupid wasp!"

He flinches but doesn't ease his grip. "I *ain't* a smart man, but I'm smart enough to know going up that fence is plain suicidal, so mebbe I'm smarter than you, raptor boy."

Suicidal. I swallow. That's the word I've been avoiding. "It *ain't.*" But my voice comes out thin and weak. "Not...not if it's an *escape attempt.*"

"And you call *me* stupid?"

It's my turn to flinch. I sag in his grip as my strength and resolve and the adrenalin all drain away together, leaving me shaking.

"Hey, don't cry, kid. Everyone will—"

"Cry? You think I feel safe enough to *cry?*"

"Oh, yeah, a hunter-born. You ain't gonna cry. Come on." He rotates us around and sits me on the bleacher with my back to the fence. "The guards are staring. Can I let go?"

He cautiously eases his bear-hug, transferring his vice-like grip to my wrist instead. But I just sit and shake, rocking to and fro slightly.

"Hey, you, uh, you've got one of those bead-things in your pocket, right?"

"My rosary?"

"Yeah, that. Heard of a team chaplet?"

"A what?" Since he's making encouraging gestures, I fish Dad's rosary out with my free hand. My trembling hand.

"I was working as an assistant way back, before I bought a share in Seb's 'Vi, and I got injured during a recovery one day. Laid up at this hunter-born camp while my leg healed. This old guy would come in every day and make me pray them beads with him. He taught me all different ways. I've forgotten most of 'em, but we could give the team one a go."

"You'll have to tell me what it is."

"Sure. It's just a standard chaplet of Saint Des, but it's when you've only got the one set of beads. Everyone grabs hold of a section, so you can have up to five join in."

I think I get the idea. I want to curl up in a ball and die, but a chaplet is probably a better idea, even some weird half-remembered thing of Wilhelm's. "Okay."

"Joshua?" Sekakuku's voice is sharp as he hurries toward us, his gaze on the tight grip Wilhelm still has on my wrist. "You okay?"

I can't quite bring myself to nod. Cold and nausea bubble inside. I wanna get on with the chaplet.

"Kid was about to get cozy with that fence." Wilhelm eyes Sekakuku warily but don't release me.

"Joshua?" Sekakuku grabs my shoulder—the bad one. He lets go when I wince. "Why didn't you tell us you were feeling off again?"

I stare at the rosary Wilhelm and I are both gripping and say nothing.

"We were just gonna do a team chaplet," says Wilhelm. "Take his mind off it all."

"Aw, heck, my aunty used to make us do those," says Billy, who's wandered up in time to catch most of it.

"Wanna join in?"

Sekakuku shoots me a look. "Yeah, why not."

Billy groans loudly but goes along with it, and they settle around me more like guards than prayer partners, reaching out to grip the rosary too. We only get through two decades before Seb saunters up and raises an eyebrow at Wilhelm.

"We're just doing a team chaplet," Wilhelm says quickly. "We've space for one more?"

Seb spits on the ground. "You're pathetic, Lollypop. You really believe that crap?"

"I don't. I mean...I, um..." Wilhelm's eyes dart

around at me, Sekakuku, Billy, back to Seb—he trails off.

"*Sure* you don't wanna put in a good word for yourself, Seb?" smirks Billy. "Or d'you think you don't need it?"

Seb just sneers back. "Don't pretend you're even on speaking terms with your imaginary friend, Billy. Or did you marry one of them women when I weren't looking?"

Billy starts to rise, fist still clenched around the rosary—Sekakuku grabs his shoulder just as tight.

"Of course," purrs Seb, "if you'd just made them get rid of the brats, your life would be a whole lot easier, eh?"

Billy's fists clench tighter, but he don't move this time. It's me who loses control of my tongue.

"Billy's right—you really *need* to put in a good word for yourself."

Seb laughs outright and strides away.

"Ooh, I've a nice new tool I'd like to introduce his smug face to," mutters Billy.

"Cool it," Sekakuku mutters back. "He ain't worth spending the rest of your life in jail."

"And Saint Des really wouldn't like it," I add. He probably don't like Billy's personal history much, neither, Seb ain't *wrong*, but Billy could've handled things *even worse*—Seb's right about that, too.

Billy raises an eyebrow. "So, the cub *is* still alive. You could've fooled me, boy. You keep away from that fence, you hear?"

"Sure," I whisper.

"And stop talking back to Seb before he makes you regret it."

Too late. I hate that Seb only ever seems to find me *funny*. But he don't seem to forget, neither—so mebbe Billy's right.

+

I ask to see the chaplain as soon as yard time is over. It's one of the nicer guards and when the chaplain radios back that he's free, he has me escorted there at once. Thank God, I end up back in Gen Pop later, not Psych Ward.

"That's a real nice one," I say, walking in to find a particularly fine old-style sailing ship floating in the filled shower tray, Sekakuku sitting in the chair beside with his stick legs stretched out, watching intently as he times its short voyage. "How's it doing?"

"Real good, cub. How's *you* doing?"

"I feel better. Had a good long chat with Father Timaru. I'm gonna try and be more careful."

"Good. Billy and I would feel kinda bad if the Raptor Whisperer ended up dead on our watch."

+

I've been having cereal every morning, so I can slip

80

a pinch of fresh food into my pocket for Mouse, but this morning...

"No cereal?"

"It's all gone now," says Dawn, one of the regular servers. "We'll probably have more by tomorrow."

"Oh, uh, then...oatmeal, please."

I head for the table, trying not to frown too obviously. Mouse can eat oatmeal, but it's gonna be messy to transport. Wilhelm got some of the last of the cereal, I see, as I sit down, and Seb ain't here yet. He's over in the corner of the hall, stretching the 'no mixing' rule to the breaking point, though he'd no doubt claim he were just trading something. And Sekakuku and Billy are still at the hatch taking their old guy pills.

Wilhelm also notices that we're alone. "Hey, Raptor Boy, wanna hear a joke?"

"Actually..." He's still sugaring the cereal, hasn't tipped his milk on yet. I hold up a single packet of sugar. "Trade you for a pinch of cereal?"

"A pinch? What d'you want a *pinch,* for?"

"Oh, go on."

He stares at me, clearly thinking it through. "*Just* a pinch?"

"Yeah."

"That's weird, Raptor Boy."

I glance around again. "Oh, come on, Wilhelm. Don't you want the sugar?"

"Yeah..." he says slowly. "But I'm kinda curious, now."

Aw, heck, I bet he is. What if he mentions it to Seb? Still, he always seems miserable and, let's face it, he most likely saved my life the other day. Playing with Mouse would probably cheer him up.

"You won't tell *no one*, not even Seb?"

"'Course not."

"Okay, I have a little mouse, that's all. And they've run out of cereal at the hatch."

Interest brightens his glum face. "Really? Can I see it? Is it tame?"

"Yeah, you can see him. He's real tame. He's in the cell. We can go up some time when Ku and Billy are busy down here."

His face falls slightly—he knows they don't like him—but he nods. "Here." He slides his bowl over. "Just take some. I owe you for the candy." He glances around for Seb as I transfer a little scoop into my pocket. "Wanna hear a joke?"

Not really. "Sure."

"How can you tell there's an elephant in your refrigerator?"

"I don't know."

"The door won't close!"

I muster a polite smile. Fortunately Seb is approaching, and *he* obviously don't smile politely at

Wilhelm's lame jokes 'cos Wilhelm never tells 'em when he's around.

+

I lie staring up at the ceiling, Darryl's letter resting on my chest. I've been on the bars as long as my shoulder can stand. I've played with Mouse until he fell asleep in my lap and had to be laid back in his tub like a sleeping baby. My thoughts seethe too badly to let me read, despite my best efforts to keep calm.

I still can't believe they sent Father Ben to prison for three months, just for not having told anyone what he knew about Darryl and Harry—he told me that on his last visit, as well. Unbelievable. He seems okay, though.

And the rest. I know I shouldn't dwell on it, but I can't stop thinking about it, despite what happened the other day. Not only am I forbidden to communicate with Darryl or Harry in any way—that weren't a surprise—but even *Father Ben* ain't allowed to see them now, because he's visiting me, can you believe?

And I can't see 'em even when I'm outta here. Over three years until Harry's eighteen and Darryl don't need custody no more. If she can't get it easily, how long will she have to avoid me for?

No, Josh. Think about something else. Think about something happy. Mebbe I could teach Mouse to do a few tricks. Yeah…

Click.

83

I push off the wall with a start, staring as the door slides open. What the heck? It ain't tier-time yet!

"Random search!" calls the guard. Jones, one of the harsher guys.

My chest constricts. *Outage!* Mouse! They'll find him.

I jump down off my bunk and stand tensely. What do I do?

Sekakuku swings his legs out of his bunk, rubbing his eyes blearily, woken from a post-lunch nap, while Billy stares grimly from where he sits at the desk. His tools are tucked under the cloth that hides them from a casual glance, but that won't help. Neither of 'em do nothing. There ain't nothing we can do.

"Outside, all three of you," says Jones.

We file out and stand along the tier, waiting. Jones and two other guards pat us down then toss the cell.

When they come back out, one of them is holding Mouse in his tub, Jones has Billy's set of tools, and the third guy holds two lighters.

"Not very good, Hunter One," says Jones, shaking his head at us. "That's four misdemeanors right here, or about ten if you count all these sharps individually, which they will. Who does all this belong to? Speak up."

"Woodworking tools are mine," growls Billy, emphasizing *tools*, though we know it won't help none.

"And that lighter."

"Other lighter's mine," says Sekakuku. "And I caught the mouse, too."

A fractional pressure of his arm against mine tells me to zip it. I don't feel good about it, but I obey. I guess he ain't *lying*. He did catch it.

"Right. It's going on your records. In you go again."

Sekakuku and Billy troop back in, but I pause in the doorway. "You'll just...chuck that mouse outside the prison, right?"

Jones shoves me in. "Dream on, hunter-boy."

Clank. Click.

I stand, staring at the mess they've left, my chest tight. No more Mouse.

"Random search, my tail," snarls Billy. "Joshua, *tell me* you didn't blab to Lollypop about that mouse of yours?"

My dismayed silence is answer enough. "You think Wilhelm told someone?" I say after a moment.

"*Someone?*" Billy rams me back against the shower screen, pinning me with an arm across my neck and jolting my shoulder. *Ouch.* "*Anything* you tell that yellow-bellied sugar junkie, you tell *Seb*, you *stupid cub!* The sooner you get that into your thick head, the better for all of us!"

"Ah, come on, Billy." Sekakuku drags his co-owner off me. "He's too trusting for his own good, but he didn't do it on purpose. He just lost something too."

"He ain't got a one hundred percent unnecessary stack of sharps misdemeanors on his record! Ain't got *nothing* on his record, after you covered for him!"

"A minor misdemeanor now ain't gonna make no difference to my chances of parole in a year or two." Sekakuku speaks in his most calming tone. "But anything would make a big difference to Josh. So cool it, Billy. This is just Seb getting his own back before he's released, that's all. The snitching snake will be gone in a week or two, tops."

"It'll take longer than that to get *this* off my record!" snarls Billy. But he marches over to the desk, stands the chair back on its legs, and throws himself into it.

I walk to my bunk, climb up, and lie down with my back to the room. Shaking. My shoulder hurts from being shoved around like that. I ain't surprised to have my suspicions about Billy's nastier side confirmed, but it don't make me happy. I've lost Mouse. And Billy's so angry with me. How could Wilhelm tell Seb when he promised not to?

Mebbe he didn't. Mebbe it *was* just a random search.

Yeah, I wish I could believe that.

+

I try to avoid Seb and Wilhelm after that, sitting on the other side of Sekakuku and Billy at meals and avoiding eye contact. I know I should forgive Wilhelm, but it's taking every scrap of effort just to keep myself together and not have any serious phobic episodes. I really, really, really don't wanna go back on those pills, and I simply don't have the energy to deal with the messed-up duo as well.

I sink into a chair in the chapel a few days later with a deep sigh of relief. A sense of peace enfolds me. Mass don't start for ten minutes, so I can just sit here and soak it up.

Father Timaru gives a short homily and I try to listen. Other things nag at my mind, sometimes stealing my attention. *Darryl...I'm in-city...pills...I'm in-city...Darryl and Harry...in-city...Wilhelm and Mouse—forget that, Josh...*

Come on, Josh. Pay attention. You're gonna be confirmed soon.

"Too often we judge others against ourselves and inevitably find them wanting," Father Timaru is saying. "Inevitably so, because they're *not* us; they are themselves. To truly love someone, we must love them as they are, not as we would like them to be. That, you may be glad to hear, is how God loves each one of us."

"Ain't much love in here, *padre*," someone mutters from a back row.

Father Timaru, experienced with hecklers, simply aims a stern look at the offender. "Trust me, there is just as much love in here as you *allow* there to be." And he moves swiftly on to the next part of Mass before things can turn into a debate.

When I get to lunch, Sekakuku and Billy sit in their usual places and Wilhelm sits alone in *his* usual place, shoulders hunched. Seb's nowhere in sight, despite the fact that I'm late after finding it hard to tear myself away from the chapel. I scan the tables. "Where's the snitch?"

Sekakuku shrugs. Billy expresses how much he don't care by not responding at all.

I glance at Wilhelm, whose wary gaze keeps running around the hall. So he betrayed me and lost me Mouse and I'd never have done that to him, but Father Timaru's right. That's just how he is.

"Where's Seb?" I ask him.

He looks up, eyes brightening 'cos I'm actually speaking to him. "Gone."

"Gone? You mean..." A grin spreads across my face. "City-folk finally made good and let him out?"

Wilhelm nods, smiling like he's not quite sure if he's happy or not. His eyes dart around nervously again. One of the biggest bullies among the city-guys is openly eyeing him up.

"You'd better sit with us from now on," I say. "You can't sit over there by yourself."

Billy's head jerks around toward me and he scowls, but I think Sekakuku gives him a kick under the table.

"Cool it, Billy. The cub's right. We let him sit with us, or we end up in a fight when someone thinks he's fair game."

"Heck, I wish we *could* leave him as fair game," mutters Billy, who seems to have done the hunter-thing and forgiven me, more or less, but he mebbe thinks he don't have to forgive city-borns quite the same. But he says nothing more as Wilhelm slides his tray along and settles into the seat beside Sekakuku, looking more cheerful than I've ever seen him.

"Hey, Raptor Boy, wanna hear a joke?"

No, I wanna sit here quietly and eat my lunch.

I'm saved from answering when Hurst, one of the senior guards, stops at the top of the table.

"Hunters, there are four of you now and we don't allow single occupancy. What are the pairs going to be?" He points to me and then to Wilhelm. "The kid and the lollypop man?" He turns his finger to Sekakuku and Billy. "Or do we split you two up?"

Billy shoots a mean look at Wilhelm, who grimaces. Heck, if those two end up sharing... It ain't nice to split up a pair of co-owners, anyway. Not ones that get along. I'd have applauded if they'd split up *Seb and Wilhelm*, only they didn't seem to notice there were any need.

"I guess it's me and Wilhelm, then," I say.

Sekakuku shoots me a worried look. "You sure?"

"What else?"

He frowns but says nothing more. Yeah, he ain't ready to be split up from his old familiar, not just for the mad cub.

+

Wilhelm watches me as I unpack, his expression shifting back and forth between wary and hopeful. This cell don't smell near as nice as Hunter One. The stench of sugar does obscure worse odors, but sugar's a tasty scent that puts my nerves on edge. I'll have to give the place a deep clean as soon as I can get my own bottle of vinda.

I'm just arranging my bedding on the spare top bunk when the door clanks and clicks closed. I climb up and settle myself. Mebbe I'll read my Bible for a bit, get ready for my next confirmation class. The chaplain gave me one with all the missing bits in.

Wilhelm rips the wrapper off a lollypop and sticks it in his mouth. "Wanna hear a joke?"

Uh-oh.

+

After supper Wilhelm unfolds the exercise bars and starts pumping it good. He's been hiding some serious muscle under his prison-orange. No wonder I couldn't get away from him in the yard. He could've broken Seb like a twig if he chose to.

After an hour, he's still sweating at it.

"You gonna give me a go on there any time soon?" I joke.

His drops back to the ground at once. "I'm sorry. I didn't mean to hog them—"

"Hey, relax," I say quickly. "You weren't hogging 'em, you were just using 'em. I was joking. You wanna use 'em longer, go for it."

But he don't move to resume his work-out. Darn. He assumes he's in the wrong about *everything*, don't he? How does a guy this big and strong get like this? Has anyone ever been nice to him? Said a word of praise? Thanked him?

Once he's rinsed the sweat off and reloaded his mouth with another lollypop, he's eyeing me again.

"Wanna hear a joke, Raptor Boy?"

I close my eyes, clinging to my patience. Only seven months to go, right? Ha ha. "Sure."

"Why can't you hear a pter-o-saur using the bath-room? Because the 'p' is silent!" Wilhelm has to take his lollypop out for a moment, he's laughing so hard.

I muster a chuckle. "Yeah, that's a classic." Pterosaurs. Huge, very sharp beaks. Much as I love 'saurs, I'm kinda glad the scientists got stopped before they could let *those* loose. How would you enjoy a jog or a swim if one of those might be about to swoop on you?

No. Don't think about jogging and swimming, wilderness, freedom... No.

"Here's another," says Wilhelm, and I wrench my mind onto what he's saying, listening good. "Can you name ten dinosaurs in ten seconds?"

"Sure, you timing? Raptor, rex, steg, allo, tri, orni, piranha, rodo, leggy, ducko-saur."

His mouth drops open. "You ain't meant to be able to do it! The answer is 'Yes, one spinosaur and nine velociraptors!'"

"Oh, sorry," I grin.

+

"*Short-circuiting fences*, what did that?" No sooner do I remove my t-shirt for my own workout, Wilhelm's on his feet, bug-eyed as he asks the inevitable question.

"Juvenile rex."

"*Holy gunsmoke!*"

I spend the next few days being accosted by random inmates demanding to see my rex bite or straight-up refusing to believe it exists. Wilhelm hangs his head each time it happens, and Billy keeps shoving him harder and harder and saying things like, "You really are a blabber-mouth, ain't you?" "Is there anyone in this whole darn place you didn't tell?" "What about *no mixing*, huh?"

Eventually I actually have to take my t-shirt off and give the whole *misfiring* wing a quick look to quell a 'let's lynch the lying hunters' riot.

I try very hard not to get angry with Wilhelm, 'cos I

can tell he's sorry.

"He'll do it again," warns Sekakuku.

"I know." I do know—now. I was a total fool to tell Wilhelm about Mouse. He'll blab whatever he thinks will most please the person he's talking to.

+

An inmate coughs, disturbing the silence. The sun is up, but the prison ain't. I find it so hard to sleep in the daytime. I'm not even trying.

My mind drifts back to the wintry mountains...

Riley fires.

Pointless to shout "NO" though I really wanna. I'm too busy trying to get the matriarch's mate in my sights as he bolts back toward the ravine. He leaps just as I fire, a split second too late—he spasms and falls, screeching in pain. But he's up, lurching forward into the shelter of the crags before I can hit him again. The other big female staggers, struck by an impressive body shot from Darryl—head was already out of sight—but she runs on too. Darn it!

I concentrate on hitting as many of the remaining raptors as I can, but they're panicking, leaping, zigzagging, the worst possible conditions for making clean kills—or any kills at all. Another one springs just as I fire, getting away totally unscathed.

Moments later, it's over. Not a raptor in sight—not up on its feet, anyway. The matriarch thrashes and screeches on the windswept rocks beside the 'Vi—Riley didn't manage a clean kill even at point-blank range. Darryl puts a bullet in its head just as I'm trying to get a clean shot. Only four other raptors lie dead in the scant snow. So that makes five dead and seven escaped, at least two badly wounded.

"Why did you fire?" I turn on Riley, angrier than I can remember being for some time. "Why, you idiot?"

He's shaking, clutching his rifle like a teddy bear... "And for pity's sake put on your safety catch," I snap. "What's the matter with you? We're inside a darn HabVi!"

Finn eases the rifle from Riley's hand, snapping the safety on and looking from me to his friend like he ain't sure whether to defend him or have a go at him too.

"Ugh, why did I even agree to this?" I sink back into my chair, my anger all for myself, now. Sure, city-groups on hunting trips are usually incompetent as heck, you expect that. That's why you only take 'em if your own crew ain't just fully trained but proper experienced. In case it all goes wrong. But Darryl and Harry ain't neither and I knew that.

Too late now.

"Now what?" asks Harry uncertainly.

"Now," I say grimly, "I'm taking these three fools out there to finish off the rest of the pack. And you and Darryl are staying right here."

Deathly silence envelops the 'Vi.

"No," says Riley, shaking his head wildly. "No, I ain't going out there!"

"This is your fault!" I snap, then break off, shaking my

own head. "No, it's mine, for being stupid enough to let you guys hunt. Fine, stay here. You ain't gonna be no use, no how. I'll take Finn and Nando."

"No." This time, it's Darryl's voice. She's on her feet, staring at me, face more inflexible than I've ever seen it. "No, Josh. You are not going out there with only those two at your back. I'm coming with you."

That guy starts coughing again, snapping me back to the unwelcome present.

Darryl, how are you? When can I see you?

Someone else curses at the cougher to shut up. Making someone yell at *him*.

All still trying to sleep, though it's past dawn. City-guys, huh?

+

"You okay?" Wilhelm eyes me from his bunk.

I press my hands to my forehead, trying to breathe steady. "Yeah, I'm just feeling a bit...squeezed."

"Squeezed?"

"By the city."

"Oh, you're *pho-bic*, right." Wilhelm pronounces the word carefully then sucks his lollypop for a moment before eyeing me again. "Wanna lollypop?"

"Uh, not right now, thanks."

He sucks his lollypop some more then suggests, "Wanna play bounce-it-off-the-walls?"

That catches my attention. "Yeah, let's."

It's a straightforward game where you bounce a ball off any wall—or anything—in the cell (*everything* is unbreakable from the shower screen to the light fittings) and each try to get it into the other's bunk space. I've played it a few times with Billy but he tires of it real quick, which is a shame 'cos having to focus like that really takes my mind off things and I can't spend long on the bars yet. The physio ordered me equally sternly to neither neglect my special exercises *nor* to overdo other things.

But I can mostly use my good side to play ball, and Wilhelm don't bore easily. When he's telling jokes, that's a nightmare—but it turns out it's real helpful with a ball game. We can play for *hours*, until I'm tired enough that my phobia stops gnawing at the back of my neck and actually allows me to lie quietly and read, while he flops down and gets out another lollypop and stares at the ceiling.

He's got a big smile on his face today, as he does just that. "Wanna lollypop, Raptor Boy?"

"Sure, thanks, Bear." I find I have to accept quite a few or it hurts his feelings, but he ain't that great at rationing himself, so I stash most of 'em so that when he runs out I can start giving 'em back.

"You look happy."

"Yeah." He gives his lollypop a couple of big licks, bottom to top, before saying, "I just like sharing a cell with you. I feel like a different person—so much nicer, y'know? I just wish I could feel this with Seb."

I swallow back the first hot words that rise to my lips. He's co-owned a 'Vi with Seb for eight years, it don't sound like either of them have any family to speak of, and I only turned up here a month or two back. If I charge in and announce that Seb's a monster who treats him like a slave, I don't know how he'll react. I guess I need to come at it sideways. Make it far less...personal.

"Actually, I wanted to tell you something," I say carefully.

"You do?"

"Yeah. You know I didn't hang out with you and Seb much, before?"

His face tenses and he sits up on his bunk. "I am real sorry about the mouse. I guess Billy's right; I am a blabber-mouth..."

I wave this away with my still-wrapped lollypop. "Yeah, I were cheesed off, but that wasn't why I avoided you guys. What I'm trying to say is, it weren't really you I were avoiding, so much. I were avoiding Seb. 'Cos, whenever I were talking to Seb, when I said something friendly, innocent, just making conversation, y'know? He always twisted whatever I said around right away and made it seem like I'd said something mean to him, like I weren't a very nice person. And it ain't right that he try to make people feel like that. He were doing it to Ku and Billy too; that's why they didn't like him much neither."

Wilhelm takes his lollypop out of his mouth and gives me a tired smile, for once looking his age. "Say, you sweet little cub, are you eeeeever so gently trying to break it to me that Seb is a mean, manipulative scumbag?"

"Uh..." Caught, I have to say, "*Yeah?*"

"Well, relax. Even a thicko like me can't spend eight years living and working with the guy and not figure that out."

"You know?" Heat floods my cheeks and I feel like a total kid. "I'm sorry, it's just...whenever he started twisting what you said, it just...it seemed like it bothered you so I figured—I figured you *believed* him."

Wilhelm pauses halfway through returning the lolly to his mouth and stares glumly at it instead. After a moment, he says, "Look, kid, a small part of me"—he taps his head with his free hand—"knows what Seb is, 'kay? It's just the bigger part of me"—he gestures vaguely to his chest—"ain't quite caught up to the trail yet. It took me so long to figure him out—I guess part of me still cares what he thinks. It's stupid, but that's me, ain't it? Thick." He shoves the lollypop back into his mouth and sucks fiercely.

"That's Seb talking," I say.

He flops down on his bunk, staring at the ceiling. "I'm thick, Josh," he says around his lollypop, his voice bleak. "Thick and spineless. You said it yourself. And Saint Des don't like lying; ain't that what you hunter-borns say? So don't try and tell me different."

It is kinda true—but I still feel a strong desire to punch Seb in his smug face.

+

"What y'doing?" Wilhelm peers over my shoulder as I carefully write out the alphabet. "That's real fancy writing."

"It's called cursive. Darryl taught me, but I ain't very neat yet. I wanna practice and surprise her." Okay, I don't have any idea when I can actually see her. But I wanna finish learning this properly, anyway, and thinking about how delighted Darryl will be makes me feel good inside.

Wilhelm stares as I write x, y, z. "What's it for?"

"It's how people used to write before they invented computers. It ain't as clear as just writing the letters individually, the way we do now. But it's quicker if you're writing loads and loads, all by hand."

"Oh."

"You wanna learn?"

"*Nah.*" His response is immediate and oddly vehement for a guy who's usually so eager to please. But he keeps coming to look over my shoulder as though fascinated by it. *Hmm.*

"D'you know how you learn to write cursive?" I say at last.

"How?" He sounds unusually closed. Un-encouraging.

"You go right back to basics and learn how to make each letter. Because people often write 'em any old way, nowadays, but to write cursive you have to be writing it *exactly* the right way so you can join 'em up proper. So, for example, this is the right way to do a 'B.'" I write a B in slow motion, then I add little arrows, the way Darryl did when she was teaching me. "And here's an 'e.' That's an easy one. And 'a.' And there's 'r.' Why don't you try?"

Panic widens his eyes as I slide the pen firmly into his hand, pressing him into the chair in my place. "Go on. Just follow the arrows."

He peers real hard at the letters before finally putting the pen nib on the paper, his tongue clamped between his teeth. Slowly, laboriously, he makes a 'B,' an 'e,' an 'a,' an 'r.' He finishes, breathing heavily, and shoots me a fearful look. I pretend not to notice anything odd.

"There, see. That's all there is to learning cursive."

"But that ain't cur-sive."

"No, but what I'm saying is that ninety percent of cursive is learning how to make the letters *just right*.

Learning how to join them up is the quick bit. Okay, after that there's practicing to get it neat. But you see what I mean. You wanna learn?"

He eyes what he's written, his gaze skittering between fear and a pride so strong that it confirms my suspicion—he can't write. Not by hand. And he's real ashamed of anyone finding out—but real tempted by the thought of learning it secretly.

Finally, he shoots another look at me, a measuring look. Deciding if he can trust me?

He takes a deep breath. "Yeah, I wanna learn."

+

I kick Wilhelm in the ankle, 'cos it's time to stand for the Eucharistic prayer. He jerks awake with a grunt and gets to his feet. Why does he even bother coming to Mass? He naps through most of it. I was pleased when he said he wanted to come, but...

Aw, no, that's why he's here, ain't it? The only reason. Seb despises religious stuff, so he didn't used to come. I'm into it, so he does.

"Wilhelm, do you *wanna* come to Mass?" I ask him, the next day.

He looks up, surprised. "Sure..."

"No, do *you* actually *wanna* go to Mass. Or are you just coming 'cos you think it makes me happy?"

He stares at me for a moment. "Don't it?"

"Only if you actually wanna come 'cos you wanna

101

come to *Mass*. It don't mean much otherwise."

He frowns, like I'm giving him a headache. Heck, trying to get him to actually decide what *he* wants to do is like drawing teeth from a live raptor.

"What do *you* actually wanna do?"

His eyes slide sideways. "Mebbe...mebbe I'll stay here today?"

"Okay," I say calmly. "I'll see you later, then." I head for the door.

He stares after me, like he can't quite believe I didn't get mad at him.

+

"You aren't seriously going out there, are you?" Riley demands, glaring at his friends.

"First rule of hunting, isn't it?" says Finn seriously, adjusting a borrowed ammo sash. "You don't leave injured animals to suffer."

"Animals? Did you see the size of them?"

Fed up with the bickering, I turn away and sip my coffee, taking advantage of what may be the last break any of us have for a while. On the 'Vi's photo frame, five-year-old me stands on one leg, holding up the other foot to show off the new boots Dad and Uncle Z just bought me at the Midsummer Fair: "'Cos you've outgrown them again."

Yeah, I remember that year...

The hot summer sun hits the back of my head, hard, and my new boots scuff in the dust, but I don't care. I'm too busy calling to the raptor, my best imitation of a young chick. The Dakotaraptor thrusts his head against the wooden rails, peering curiously down at me. They only ever use full-adult raptors for rodeo so he's old enough to have done plenty of baby-sitting duties even if he ain't mated, yet.

He makes a wary crooning noise, unsure whose nestling I am. I reply fluently. Yeah, he's being real friendly, thinks I'm a harmless chick, which I am. Mebbe if I ask him real nicely, he'll let me climb right onto his back! I need to make friends first, though...

Peeping sweetly, I scramble up onto the first rail and reach in, trying to touch his face through the muzzle...

"Josh, no!"

Uh-oh, it's Dad! I'm grabbed and plucked from the rail. Soon I'm walking beside Dad through the fair, back on my baby reins—Dad's holding 'em real tight—Uncle West walking with us. Apparently everyone else is still "looking for me." Brey Fischer, almost six, and a whole year older than I am, laughs at my reins from across the pathway. I scowl.

"Gonna to sulk for the rest of the fair, Josh?" demands Dad. "Because the reins aren't coming off again this year so you may as well give it up. You just had your chance to be a big boy and not wander off and you blew it."

"Never did I see a chance as blown as that," mutters Uncle West.

"Josh! You found him, thank Saint Des!" Uncle Z strides towards us, his eyes on me. "Where was he?"

"Where would you expect?" drawls Uncle West.

"Climbing into a raptor pen," says Dad, more helpfully.

Uncle Z draws in a sharp breath, leaning to put his face closer to mine. "Joshua Wilson, you should know better than that! Those rodeo raptor have bare wing claws and weigh a third of a ton. You should be spanked into next week!"

A spark of hope stirs. "Yeah! Spank me good and then no reins?"

For some reason all three of them just roar with laughter.

"That kid ain't dumb," says Uncle West.

Dad leans to look at me too, his face stern. "Reins, Josh."

My heart sinks. But a screechy cry from the rodeo pens distracts me. "Dad, when can I ride one?"

"When you're older. A lot older."

My heart sags again.

"Ah, come on, Josh, cheer up." In the next moment he's hefted me up and deposited me on his shoulders. "You can ride me.*"*

Grinning, I reach for his hair, to grip it for balance...but just before I can touch it he evaporates like morning mist and I plummet, hitting the dusty floor, hard... Ouch.

"Dad?" I look up, my eyes searching frantically, but Dad's nowhere in sight and Uncle Z and Uncle West are gone too. Fernanda Matthews leans over me, lips pursed, her neat turquoise clothes pristine. Horribly artificial apple scent fills my nose.

"Those little reins aren't nearly enough for a wild thing

like you," she tuts. "This won't do at all."

*She reaches out…*click…click…click…click… *Cold metal bracelets fasten around my wrists, my ankles. Short lengths of chain join them to a belt around my waist. I yank, trying to get free, but it's hopeless.*

"No! Dad, where are you? Dad, help me!" But there's just Fernanda, smiling and nodding to herself. "No! Take these off me!" Trapped! Can't get free! Panic explodes inside me. "Please? Please let me go! Daaaaad!"

"Hey, kid, wake up…"

My shoulder twinges as someone shakes it. My eyes fly open.

Dim light fills the little concrete and metal room. Prison—and no Dad. Great.

Wilhelm stands beside my bunk. Sweat coats me and my heart's hammering after that horrible awakening. I try to stop gasping and breathe normally.

"You okay, Raptor Boy?" He grips my good shoulder this time.

"Yeah, sorry I woke you. Just a bad dream." As he moves back toward his bunk, I can't help adding, "Bad at the end, anyway. I were dreaming about my dad and he vanished. It were horrible."

"Your dad's dead, right?" His bunk creaks as he vaults back up onto it.

"Yeah. Five years ago. I miss him every day. He were the best dad in the world."

Five years. How can it have been that long? Huh, I think of Wilhelm as being older than Dad but actually, if Dad had lived, he'd be about Wilhelm's age now. Weird thought.

Silence from Wilhelm. Surely he can't have fallen back to sleep already?

No, because — suddenly — he says, "Happiest day of my life was when I was eighteen and that hunter said he'd give me a try and we drove off outta the city. I've never seen my dad since."

My heart twists. "Never? You didn't get along?"

"Heck, no. I think he killed my mom when I were five, though everyone said she fell down the stairs. But he was always hitting us — my little sister and me — and…and hurting us. Eventually it got so bad I called the cops one night. They came and took my sister away — I never saw her ever again. But they left me there." His deep voice sounds so small in the darkness. "I never could figure out why they left me. Mebbe 'cos I was a boy — but surely they know that —" He breaks off. "*Misfire*, why am I telling you this? I've never told anyone about this. Almost anyone. Don't…don't tell no one? *Please?*"

"Of course not." My throat feels tight; I just dunno what to say. "I'm real sorry, Wilhelm, that your dad were so mean."

He lets out a shaky breath. "Heck, I'm not sure you

even understand what I'm on about. Sweet little hunter-born cub that you are, with your wonderful dad and everything." He sounds more sad than envious.

I frown into the darkness. I feel like mebbe I am missing something in this conversation, but I really, really don't wanna say the wrong thing.

"Wilhelm," I say softly, "I can't pretend to know what it was like for you, having a dad like that, 'cos I can't even *imagine* my dad hurting me. But even *trying* to imagine Dad hurting me is so bad that...that I really feel for you. I'm glad your sister got saved, and I'm so sorry you didn't and...and I'm glad you got that hunting job."

He's silent for a moment, then he just whispers, "Thanks, Josh."

It's a long time before either of us sleep again.

+

"Had fun?" Wilhelm eyes me doubtfully when I get back from my confirmation class.

"Yeah." I climb up onto my bunk and flop. I can't believe it's August already. "Only a couple of weeks now until the big Mass! We learned about purgatory today. How nothing impure can be with God, so you gotta get clean first, and yeah, it really hurts but it's better than going to hell forever."

Wilhelm shudders. "Ugh, purgatory, hell, that's all heavy stuff. Who would even wanna think about that?"

I shrug. "Well, anyone who don't wanna go there, mebbe? I almost landed before God real unprepared; I ain't making that mistake twice."

Wilhelm rips the wrapper off a soft lollypop and shoves it in his mouth. He chews on it hard for a while, before finally saying, "Mebbe it ain't even true."

"You like that idea better?"

He chomps on the lolly some more. "Dunno," he says at last. "Ain't much of a choice."

After a while, he asks, "You wanna hear a joke?"

+

"Stop, Seb. Stop! We've gotta stop! Please, Seb! We've gotta go back. We've *gotta*! Seb, *please*! Please don't do this! *Please...*"

Wilhelm's twisting and turning, babbling in his sleep. It ain't the first time he's gone on like this. He's always asking Seb to stop, to not make them do something, to go back, that kinda thing. This time, it seems so bad and it's going on so long I finally slip down from my bunk and shake his arm. He starts awake, recoiling against the wall.

"Hey, relax, Bear. You were having a nightmare."

"I'm sorry!" He wraps his arms around his head, like he's expecting me to hit him. "I'm sorry I woke you..."

"It's okay." I pat his muscley shoulder until he gradually uncurls, lowering his arms. "You okay?"

"Yeah. Yeah. I'm sorry I woke you..."

"Hey, I wake you with nightmares too. Don't worry about it."

+

I suck on a lollypop as I sit on the bleachers with Wilhelm, watching two gangs of city-guys swirling around on the other side of the yard.

"Think it's gonna kick off?" I ask Wilhelm, since he knows city-guys better than I do.

He shrugs, not bothering to take his lolly out as he answers, "It could anytime. Them Elders of yours know what they're doing, telling us to stay out of it all."

That sure is true. The no mixing rule can come across as harsh and it sure is socially limiting, but it saves hunters in jail a whole lotta grief in the long run.

The guards in the towers are watching as well, I can see from the direction of their silhouettes. Are we gonna lose the rest of our yard-time? If—or rather whenever— a fight happens out here, they fire into the ground and every inmate has three seconds from 'shots fired' to get down flat on the ground, then the guards will shoot anyone still up. Theoretically. There's a real old guy who probably couldn't get down flat in less than one minute who just sits right where he is on the bleachers and puts his hands up and his head down, and they ain't shot him yet.

But after 'shots fired,' everyone has to line up and

go straight back in, no more fresh air, which cheeses everyone off, so premeditated fighting tends to be an indoor activity. Of course, with the self-control of the average city-guy, let alone the average city-guy *in here*, unpremeditated fights ain't exactly uncommon, and there sure does look like one brewing. At least we can just sit over here and keep out of it, 'cos everyone knows *hunters don't mix*.

Sekakuku moves to the lowest bleacher, clearly in preparation for getting his slightly creaky joints down on the ground as easily as possible, then goes straight back to arguing with Billy about boats.

"Oh, *misfire*, they're off," mutters Wilhelm, as the first punch gets thrown and the two groups turn into a seething mob of fists and orange.

Us hunters are hitting the deck even as the sharp retort of the shots echoes back from the walls. We lie there as the guards wade in among the now horizontal mob and start deciding who to drag off to solitary and who to cart off to Medical and who to just straight-up yell at.

"When them shots are fired, you ever just think about standing there and doing nothing?" says Wilhelm from beside me, in an unusually bleak voice.

I twist my head to peer at him, the back of my neck prickling coldly. "Yeah, I used to think about it all the time, but I don't no more. You shouldn't, neither."

What little of his face I can see at that angle brightens. "Oh, I don't think about it anymore. Not since Seb left."

"Good," I mutter. I've barely thought about it since Seb left, neither, come to think. Sekakuku and Billy were nice enough to me, but they just did their own thing, mostly. But now, if I look at all unoccupied, Wilhelm wants to interact. Which is real annoying, sometimes, but—I guess it's been protecting me from myself more than I realized.

+

"Why are *you* beaming like an idiot?" demands Billy, as Wilhelm settles at the lunch table with a big grin on his face. "Oh, wait, you are one."

Wilhelm's grin slips and he glances down at his plate.

"What's up, Bear?" I ask.

The grin comes back. "Some guy just gave me a whole bag of candy for writing a card to his wife real nice. Wanted it done in 'that real fancy writing you do.'" He makes quote marks, the grin widening even more.

No wonder he's so proud. A month ago he couldn't even write. He has worked real hard at it.

"Hmm," says Sekakuku. "Mebbe I should get one of you two to write my daughter's birthday card."

Ku has two grown-up kids, it turns out. His wife

died when they were little, and he left them with her sister to be raised at her camp. Which may be why he ain't on speaking terms with his son, the eldest. But his daughter writes to him now and then, and he writes back.

A few days later, a city-guy asks if I'll teach him "fancy writing" in exchange for a lighter. I don't wanna lighter, 'cos it's a misdemeanor if found, but Wilhelm wants it, so I agree. After all, without a trade, it would break the *no mixing* rule.

We get a steady stream of work after that—Wilhelm does the cards, I do the teaching. *Hunter Two Fancy Writing Ltd*, we jokingly call it. I can always tell which guys can't actually write—most of 'em, that's why they've come to me—but I pretend I don't notice, just like with Wilhelm. I think most of 'em arrange to retake their Literacy Test, though most don't admit it.

I suspect Wilhelm retakes the test, 'cos he disappears for an hour one morning, but for once he keeps quiet about his achievement. I'm betting *someone* he did previously trust with the fact that he was only RT mocked him so badly he just can't bear anyone else to find out. Ever. He *can* keep a secret—if it's important enough to him.

+

"Wanna hear a joke?"

"I gotta do this, Bear." It's my second to last

confirmation class later today, and I'm supposed to be reading part of the third chapter of Genesis.

He sighs and digs into a bag of candy. Guess he's eaten all his lollypops this week.

I read for a while. "That's interesting," I say eventually.

"What is?"

"Y'know what the *second* sin was?"

"Huh?"

"The first was listening to someone other than God and disobeying him, obviously. But the second...listen: *'God asked Adam, "Have you been eating of the tree I forbade you to eat?" The man*—that's Adam—*replied, "It was the woman you put with me; she gave me the fruit, and I ate it."' That* was the second sin."

"You have totally lost me, kid." Wilhelm speaks flatly.

"Adam tried to *shift the blame.* His wife tried to persuade him to do something he knew was wrong, right? He shoulda said no. But he didn't. And it don't matter how much she tried to pressure him or manipulate him or if she cried at him, even. All that affects *exactly* how guilty he were, but it don't change the fact that he were. Guilty. He had free will and he coulda said no. But when God challenged him, he tried to blame his wife. And when God challenged *her,* she tried to blame the snake. Sin number two. Make sense?"

"Sheesh, that is *heavy*, kid. What you even wanna think about all that for?" He drags a magazine from under his pillow and opens it.

I jot a few things in my notepad, trying to ignore what he's holding, though it makes me real uncomfortable. I've seen him tucking it away out of sight when I get back to the cell from time to time, so I can guess what it is.

"Y'know," I say at last, after re-reading the passage. "Seems like Adam was probably the 'Vi-boss—well, garden-boss—right? D'you think if *he'd* said no, it woulda been no on behalf of the whole 'Vi—or human race, in this case? And Eve woulda just fallen *personally*, but nothing more?"

"Eve?" says Wilhelm grumpily. "*Wait up...*" He rifles through several pages, folds the cover back and tosses the magazine into my lap. "Why doncha take a good look at *Eve* and chill, kid?"

I grab the magazine and lob it to the floor, but I've caught a glimpse that'll burn in my brain for days. *Great.* Bad enough that I had that *mortifying* dream about Darryl the other week.

"*No, thanks*, Wilhelm."

I've never *seen* what I saw in that dream and I don't wanna until she's my... I choke off that presumptuous thought. I can hope, right?

"Hey, you don't hafta crumple it all up like that..."

objects Wilhelm.

"You chuck that filth at me, and I'll darn well chuck it on the floor where it belongs!"

"Ooh, the cub does have a temper after all! Sheesh, you hunter-borns can be so up-tight sometimes." Wilhelm drops down from the bunk to grab the magazine. "Though I got this from *Ku*, I'll have you know."

I pick up my Bible and try to concentrate on it.

"*Grown* men have needs, y'know," Wilhelm adds nastily.

I put the Bible down again. "The *heck they do*, Bear. That's the oldest lie in the book; you don't really believe it, do you? Anything your body *needs*, it'll take care of, you can be sure of that. Anything *you* do while you're awake, that's not *need*, that's just *want*, and you can't be a man with proper self-control and not be in charge of *that*."

"That's hunter-born crap," snaps Wilhelm.

"That's the truth. Keep that thing away from me or I'll get a lighter just so I can burn it. How'd you like it if your sister were in there?"

Wilhelm tenses, pushing half off the bunk, a dangerous look in his eyes, and for once I remember how strong he is. "My sister ain't in there!"

I ain't backing down. "Yeah? How would you know? And why's it okay for *other* guys' sisters to be in there, if it ain't for *yours*?"

Wilhelm remains still, breathing heavily. Eventually, still not saying anything, he makes a real big thing of settling back on the bunk and opening up the magazine again and making himself comfortable.

Struggling for calm, I turn back to my Bible and re-read the first sentence three times without taking it in.

"You *misfiring* spoilsport of an up-tight hunter-born *pup*!" Wilhelm leans down, opens his locker, shoves the magazine inside, and slams the door loudly. He throws himself back on the bed, folding his muscley arms. After a moment, he unfolds them long enough to chuck a huge handful of candies into his mouth and start crunching them hard, glaring at the ceiling.

Hiding a smile, a rush of relief going through me, I keep my attention focused on the text in front of me. Too much to hope Wilhelm will never look at that thing again—I don't reckon it's that easy for guys to stop when they're used to it—but at least he's put it down, right now, today. And mebbe he'll be slower to pick it up, in the future.

+

"Stay low," I hiss, waving to Finn and Fernando to get down as they make their way up the slope. It's mostly bare rock, the snow swept away by the storm. Nice and quiet.

They drop right onto their knees to crawl the last section—good—so I turn my attention back to the raptors milling below us.

"How do we do this?" murmurs Darryl from beside me. I never, ever meant to let her out on a foot patrol until she were more experienced, but she didn't exactly give me a choice today. I am the boss, though. Surely I coulda put my foot down?

She's a hundred times more competent than either of these city-idiots, so I am glad to have her here. As far as my own skin is concerned, anyway.

I sweep the clearing with my sights, taking stock of the different Utahraptors. Seven of 'em, four still sleek-feathered and rippling-muscled, though right now circling nervously, two down and bleeding, one juvenile limping and crying pitifully, clearly as distressed by the absence of its parents and the distraction of its elders as by its injuries.

"There are two ways in and out of that den area, both of 'em ravines." I scan the surrounding landscape. "Finn and Nando can cover the one on the left from right here. But we ain't gonna be able to get into a position to cover the one below us without falling off a precipice. So you and I will have to go down and cover it from within. That's definitely more up close and personal than ideal, but if we don't stop that bolt hole, we'll never get them all."

"Okay," is all she says.

"We should be able to drop the four healthy ones all at once. That will only leave the injured ones for the second volley. As these things go, it's fairly safe and *straightforward."*

"Good."

I switch my attention to Finn and Fernando. "Are you guys up to this?"

More sober-faced than I've yet seen them, they nod wordlessly. Riley's back at the 'Vi with Harry—Riley relieved, Harry furious, but at least he's safe. Unlike Darryl...

Stop it, Josh. Darryl's old enough to make her own choices.

Not according to the city-folk, but what do they know? I've met people twice her age who ain't half as fit to make their own decisions as she is.

"Fire as soon as we do," I tell them. "Take the two closest to you and make sure you each know which one is yours. Don't fire before. Not unless you see something sneaking up on us or you, anyways."

More nods. "Okay. Come on, Darryl, let's move."

We make our way down the boulder-strewn slope and into the crags surrounding the den easily enough. Soon I pause, point down the ravine we're following, lay two fingers to my arm, then place my fingertip to my lips.

We're only about two hundred feet from the nests. We mustn't make a sound. Darryl nods silent understanding.

Placing my steps with painstaking care, hoping and praying Darryl's less experienced feet don't knock a rock or crunch in a patch of deep snow, I pick my way to where the ravine opens out into what's probably primarily a nursery area, but one used for much of the year as a convenient den.

Darryl eases up at my shoulder and we both raise our rifles. I touch my finger to my barrel and point to the right-hand healthy raptor. Point my finger to her and to the next raptor to the left. Another silent nod.

I'm about to fire when a yell from above brings every raptors' head swinging around. What the—?

Swiftly, I adjust my aim, but the nervy raptor springs to the side just as I fire, and I miss. Darryl's raptor drops, but there's no firing from above. Not good...

I drop the closest raptor but another rushes toward us, full-tilt. Darryl fires just as it leaps—misses. I fire...it stumbles, but springs again, carrying Darryl to the ground.

"DARRYL!" My scream mingles with hers as its claws flash, blood spraying across the rock and snow...

"Wake up, kid!"

"Huh?" I open my eyes to a dim concrete room, my chest shuddering as I gulp in air. Ugh, what a horrible dream. I'm actually glad to wake up here.

In reality, that foot patrol went like clockwork. Four healthy raptors were dropped, all at once, then the remaining three a couple of seconds later. No screams from above; no trouble at all. Not like that ghastly...

I drag my mind from the nightmare, glancing at Wilhelm, who stands there groggy-eyed and yawning. "Aw, sorry, Bear. Did I wake you? Thanks for waking me."

"I wake you up often enough. Fair's fair."

I'm shaking—hard—and drenched in sweat. I pull up my t-shirt to wipe my face, trying to get my breathing under control.

Wilhelm moves to the window and peers upward. "It's clear. You wanna show me some more stars?"

He might just be trying to distract me, but he seems to enjoy it, so with a final wipe I let my t-shirt fall and slide from the bunk, the August night air pleasantly cool on my damp skin. "Yeah." But as I crane my neck to get the best view, as usual I can't help shaking my head. "Ugh, city-lights, prison lights, it's awful. You did look at the sky sometimes at night, right? Out in the wilds?"

"Sure. I'd go up the turret occasionally and open a window. It was beeeeautiful. Did make me feel real small, though. Seb would laugh at me."

"It don't matter what Seb thinks," I say firmly.

"Yeah, he ain't here."

"Don't matter anyway," I say.

He just peers up and points. "There's the Plow and the North Star." After spending his adult life hunting, Wilhelm did know those already. "Did you say that was Venus?"

"Yep."

I stare up at the few stars that manage to make themselves seen through all the light pollution, my mind drifting back to Darryl. Darryl, alive and healthy, no blood, no screaming…

…the end of her braid brushes over the back of my hand as she bends forward to peer into the eyepiece of my telescope. I shift back to give her more space.

"Wow, what is that?" she asks. "A nebula?"

"Sure is."

"Thinking about your girl?" Wilhelm's voice jerks me back to the present.

"She ain't my—"

"Yeah, yeah, ain't your girl. But you want her to be."

I don't say nothing. Saint Des don't like lying.

+

Wilhelm comes to the confirmation Mass, as do Sekakuku and Billy. Father Ben is there, too. Afterward, there's a little party in the bare prison chaplaincy room, for me and my fellow 'confirmandi': two murderers from A-wing, and two other guys from B-wing, along with a few of our friends and family. The small room is packed, but there's a magnificent cake, donated by the prison warden, who I meet for the first time.

"Joshua Wilson, is it?" A tall, sober man in a suit who reminds me of a gray heron, he spears a small cube of his delicious cake neatly with a plastic fork and eats it. "The hunter boy?"

"Yes'sir." Huh, is it me, or is he singling me out?

121

"I hear the full literacy rates in B-wing are skyrocketing." He raises an eyebrow meaningfully.

Uh-oh. We're near the cake, so we're near Wilhelm. "That's great," I say innocently. But when he opens his mouth again, I narrow my eyes and glare at him. *Shut up.*

A slight smile crosses his lips. "Well, congratulations—on your confirmation." He toasts me with another lump of cake and moves off through the crowded room. *Phew.*

"Thanks for coming, Bear," I say, joining Wilhelm. "I know you don't really like religious stuff."

He shrugs. "It's just too heavy," he mutters. "But"—he brightens—"this *cake* is enough to make me believe in God and angels and *everything.*"

Father Ben, who's just come up to us, raises an eyebrow at that. I just about manage to hold down a laugh.

"How are you doing, Josh?" Father Ben asks. "Good?"

"Yeah. Mass was wonderful." After having that silent Friend in the 'Vi for almost a whole year, I finally got to receive Him properly. I didn't have an ecstasy or nothing, but it made me feel real warm and happy inside.

On Sunday morning, Wilhelm follows me to the cell door at Mass time.

"You coming?" I can't help sounding surprised.

He shrugs. "Realized I miss the change of scenery."

Does he? Or did I act too pleased? Or something else?

But since he just comes on Sundays, he seems to understand he don't *have* to—so I sure don't try to discourage him. He still naps through the homily.

+

It's September. Less than three months until the earliest time they might release me.

"Please, please, please, Saint Des," I whisper.

"Huh?" Wilhelm glances over at me.

"End of November, beginning of December. That's the earliest possible date they might let me out. It's getting so close."

"Oh. Yeah." He sounds glum, though. He'll be in with Sekakuku and Billy once I'm gone. I hope Billy don't give him too hard a time.

"Still better than Seb, right?" The words slip out before I can think them through.

He glances at me again, his gaze going bleak, the way it does whenever Seb is mentioned. "Yeah," he says. "Well, I don't have to worry about Seb for at least five years. I can be thankful for that much."

"You don't have to worry about Seb ever again, if you don't wanna. Why go back to him?"

He shakes his head. "Minor matter of my life

savings tied up in his 'Vi. Twenty-five percent share."

"Sell it."

"You know a co-owner has to approve any buyer. He won't let me sell. Won't risk getting someone with brains and a backbone."

"Fine. Walk away. You'll still own the share; if anything happens to Seb, you can claim it back. In the meantime, start over. Save up again."

Wilhelm shakes his head heavily. "I ain't good at saving, kid, and I'm getting worse." He pulls the lollypop from his mouth, stares at it, shakes his head and smiles sadly. "Took me fifteen years to save up just for that twenty-five percent share. And that were a bargain. The guys I were working for warned me, said Seb were offering too good a deal, but I were too greedy and impatient and *stupid* to listen. The guys told me, wait, wait for someone you know, or that *we* know, at least, but Seb seemed so charming. I shoulda listened. Now it's too late."

"It *ain't* too late. Look, Wilhelm, when you get out, you can come to me. I'll probably be able to use an assistant—and if I can't, I promise I'll find you a position in a decent 'Vi, with some good guys. I *promise*."

Wilhelm gloomily shoves his lollypop back into his mouth, speaking around it. "Kid, you're a real sweet cub, but you just don't understand how humiliating it would be for a guy my age, a *co-owner*, to be working as an *assistant*."

Especially to some young cub, hangs in the air unsaid.

"You really think that matters, compared to—" I shake my head. "Just don't go back to Seb; it ain't worth it. You shouldn't have to live like that. It's only money."

"Only money?" He pulls his lollypop out yet again and stares at me. "Kinda important, kid."

"Yeah, but there're *more* important things. Happiness, for starters. Life, for another. You ain't *living*, stuck with a guy like Seb. You're just *not dead yet*."

He's gone so still and silent I know I've hit a nerve. "We can't all be as dismissive of money as a kid who inherited a whole 'Vi," he says shortly.

"If money were everything, I *wouldn't* have inherited a whole 'Vi. I wouldn't have been born at all. My mom were gonna *kill* me. My dad had saved up half the cash for a new 'Vi—but he gave it to her, instead. Blood money. Saved me, but he were back to square one, financially."

Wilhelm stares at me, his hand falling away from his lollypop, which is stuck to the roof of his mouth. "You're kidding."

"Saint Des my witness, he did. It's the truth."

Wilhelm stares until his lollypop almost falls and he has to grab for it. "I guess all that niceness is genetic, then."

He don't say he'll come work for me, and I don't push it. Mebbe when the idea has a chance to sink in, he'll decide getting away from Seb is worth a little embarrassment after all.

+

"I am glad they should be letting you out soon," Wilhelm says, when I come into the cell after daily Mass some days later. Morning tier-time has started so the cells are unlocked. "You know that, right? I don't know anyone who deserves to be in here less than you."

"Yeah, I know that."

"Good. I know I get kinda down whenever it comes up."

"It's fine, Bear."

Hey, there's an envelope on my bed! I tip the contents out. Another angel singer. I look at it and grin. 'Big' 'fat' 'bull' 'close' 'ahead' 'friend' read the trail signs. A very hunter way of promising good times soon to come. "Thanks, guys," I murmur.

"What's it say?" asks Wilhelm, when I show it to him.

Ah, city-born, right. He don't know trail signs. They're not actually used much out hunting anymore. More common on formal wear and kids slipping notes to each other and older people writing love letters. I tell him.

He grins and goes to his locker. "On that subject, Happy Birthday, kid. I've got something for you."

My cheeks heat up. "Oh, you remembered." He did ask when it was some weeks ago but no one's mentioned it yet so I figured he forgot the date before he could tell anyone.

He laughs. "I couldn't take delivery of your gift until tier-time so the other two agreed to keep quiet. Here it is. I—" He gasps and leans his head further into the locker, examining something. "Oh no, I think—I think it's dead!"

Dead? "What is it, a mouse?"

He straightens, his face screwed up in dismay, holding a tub. "Yeah..." He pulls the lid off quickly. "Misfire, it *is* dead! It was fine before."

I take the tub, glancing at the lid in his hand as a whiff of mouse and death reaches my nostrils. A single air hole. A quick examination of the mouse tells me what I need to know. I glance into his locker. "Did you put that folded shirt on top?"

"Yeah, I didn't want it squeaking and giving the game away. Figured it's only cloth, enough air for a mouse would seep through, right?"

Not through that many layers. But I say, "I guess it blocked the air hole just a little too much."

Despite my attempt to downplay his mistake, Wilhelm swings around, slamming his clenched fists into the wall. "Why am I so thick? I'm such an *idiot!* I should just be put down like an animal, the way Seb always says. The world would be so much better off..."

"Wilhelm!" He's so upset. I'm not surprised. He clearly bought it from some guy who works in the kitchens, and it probably cost him, plus death's too significant to deal out by accident, even to an animal. I've never forgotten how I jumped down from my berth when I were a little kid and landed on a rabbit that I didn't know were loose in the 'Vi, broke its back. Heck, did I feel horrible, though it wouldn't have bothered me to wring its neck so Dad could cook it for dinner.

Wilhelm hits the wall again. "I'm an *idiot,* such an idiot!"

"Wilhelm, don't!" *Quick, Josh, how can you turn a dead mouse into a brilliant birthday gift?* I pick up the limp body—it's still warm. It's a larger species than Mouse and real plump. Been living it up in the prison kitchen, for sure. *Plump...* Bullseye. "Hey, Bear, this is great."

"Great?" He spins around, face wrinkled up in confusion.

"Yeah. What we have here is a nice fresh piece of meat, right? Have you still got those marshmallows you bought from the store?" I'd think it a slim chance, except I've not seen him eat them yet.

"Yeah. I was keeping them for today. I've saved some lolly sticks and I've got a lighter."

That explains it. "Perfect. And Ku and Billy have lighters too. So we can invite them around for a cook-out. Mouse for the main, marshmallows for dessert."

Wilhelm eyes the mouse in my hand. "It'll be, like, a mouthful each, Josh."

"So what. We'll still have prepared and cooked it ourselves. It'll be great. You in?"

"Sure...if you...if you wanna."

"Father Ben gave me something to open today. I'll take a look now in case it's food. We'd better have the cook-out during afternoon tier-time; there ain't time now."

"Okay." Wilhelm still sounds uncertain, but he's stopped punching the wall and talking about being put down, so I'll take that.

He moves to the exercise bars, folds 'em down, pulls off his t-shirt and start pumping. Hopefully it will help him calm down. "It helps me keep my head in a good place," he said once, which I totally get.

I put the mouse safely in my locker to make it clear I value the gift, odd though it is, take out the little package Father Ben gave me and rip it open.

"Huh, not edible," I say. "Fun, though. I mentioned how rubbish the star-gazing is in here. And look..."

Wilhelm drops to the ground and steps over to take a peep. "Glow in the dark stars? Hey, that's real nice of him."

"Yeah."

Wilhelm smiles suddenly. "Why don't we have a *nighttime* cookout? Arrange a blanket under the bunk there to block the light and stick the stars up? Then you won't even be able to *see* the prison."

"That's a fantastic idea, Wilhelm." My phobia's really not so bad these days, if I keep active and get to Mass, but I don't have to try hard to sound super-enthusiastic. "Let's do that!"

+

Once the cells unlock for afternoon tier-time, Ku and Billy come around carrying their mugs and their pillows to sit on, just as though they were coming to another 'Vi to socialize. Getting all four of us under the lower bunk is a squeeze, but there's just enough space. Even with the blankets hung up, it's still light enough to see, and the stars don't show up that much, but we can use our imaginations.

Billy lends his sharpest woodworking tool so I can skin and prepare the mouse. We take a leg each, sharing the three lighters around to roast the meat. It's a nice healthy mouse, so Wilhelm sharpens some cardboard lollysticks, and we use them to spike the heart and liver and teeny-weeny kidneys, cooking and eating those too.

When Wilhelm ends up with the heart, Billy opens his mouth and I can see the *mouse-hearted* jibe coming so clearly that I ruthlessly jab him in the leg with my sharp lollystick. He scowls at me, rubs his leg, but shuts his mouth again. It is my birthday, after all.

Once we've had as much mouse as we can find to eat, we move on to marshmallows. It's slow work, even with three lighters, but it's real fun getting them to crisp up just right. Plenty of laughter as people miss-time it and marshmallows burst into flames and have to be hastily blown out.

Heck, it's like being around a campfire somewhere out in the wilds—or at least in the 'Vi-park. Quite a few marshmallows later, we're still having a blast when footsteps suddenly approach rapidly, entering the cell.

"Maybe there are a couple of them under here, but where the others are—"

We just have time to hide the lighters before the blanket is yanked up.

"Oh. They are all here."

The genial older guard, Hurst, and a greenhorn peer in at us, Hurst relaxing as his nightmare vision of prisoners escaping on his watch fades away. The greenhorn's gaze falls on the remains of the mouse in the tub, and he claps a hand to his mouth.

"Ugh! It's a baby's hand! They've eaten it!"

We all turn identical looks of flat hunter incredulity on the cretin. Hurst leans closer to inspect the mess. "It's just a mouse. Look, there's the skin."

"But they ate it?"

"Looks like."

"I think I'm gonna be sick."

Hurst eyes the four of us. "I'm guessing even hunters don't eat mice raw."

Uh-oh. "Raw mouse is very juicy," I say quickly, though surely even city-guys can't miss the scent of caramelized sugar? "Uh, succulent, that's the word."

Nope. He gives me a *nice try, kid* smirk. "Produce the lighter or I'll have to toss the cell."

He ain't gonna do that anyway? He must know it's my birthday. Probably everyone does, since Wilhelm knew.

Wilhelm's already whipped out his lighter and handed it over. He knows he'll catch it if Ku and Billy lose theirs unnecessarily, let alone Billy's precious tool.

"*Thank you.*" Hurst pockets it. "Misdemeanor for you, Fenn." He eyes the mouse skeleton, then glances at me. "Just...make sure you clear all this up, the four of you."

He drops the blanket and they move away.

"They're *sick!*" the greenhorn protests. "Aren't you going to do anything?"

"Ah, get it together. You want *sick*, go do a stint in A-wing. A mouse BBQ is harmless hunter eccentricity."

"You know what they say about that kid?" The voices pause outside the cell as other footsteps move past. "A rex grabbed him by the shoulder, shook him around like a dog shaking a rat, and threw him down on the ground. But when it stamped up to eat him, he just whipped out his belt knife and slit its throat, calm as you like!"

"You're an idiot, greenhorn." Their footsteps begin to move away again. "You must *not* believe everything the cons tell you…"

I'm laughing so hard I have to bite my sleeve not to make a noise. Wilhelm's stuffed his pillow over his face, and tears of laughter are leaking from Ku's eyes. Even Billy's grinning like a loon. We all know better than to laugh our heads off—audibly—at a pair of Tazers that have just let us off real easy.

"Saint-Des-put-me-in-a-diaper," chuckles Billy, "that greenhorn ain't never tried skinning no 'saur, has he?"

"Slit that rex's throat, did you, Josh?" sniggers Ku. "You be careful of him, Lollypop. He's deadly, this cub."

Wilhelm takes the pillow away from his face at last and shrugs. "Kid probably just charmed the rex by being nice to it."

Billy snorts, eyeing Wilhelm maliciously. "What kinda present is a *dead mouse*, anyways?"

I jab him with my lollypop stick so hard it starts to bend.

"Only Joshua Wilson could get bit by a rex, *by*

accident, while riding on another rex." Ku helpfully rolls right over the mouse comment. "Why *were* you rex-riding, anyway? You were real evasive about *that*, when you told the story before. An illegal rodeo, eh?"

I already told them about Darryl and Harry's dad being kidnapped, after getting Darryl's letter and knowing it weren't a secret no more. So now I explain about how we snuck into Jason's illegal rex farm to look for William Franklyn and ended up letting all the poor mistreated rex out and having to ride three of 'em through the fence to safety.

When I've finished, Billy whistles. "And the weird thing is, I actually believe you," he says. "Almost. Kinda. Mebbe."

"I did hear something about an illegal rex farm," says Ku, scratching his upper lip thoughtfully, "shortly before we got thrown in here. There were some rumors going around."

Were there? Not among *my* circles, but anyway. I ain't in no doubt that Ku and Billy run with a rougher crowd. I'm lucky they're decent enough to take responsibility for a young cub rather than just push him around, though I reckon the fact that the 'Raptor Whisperer' is a teen-weeny celebrity in hunter circles didn't hurt.

Wilhelm shakes his head glumly. "I'm sorry you didn't find him there, kid. Especially since you got bit like that and ended up in here."

I shrug. "Yeah, well, it's pretty clear he's dead. Which is awful for Darryl and Harry, but we did do our best to find him."

Wilhelm still looks sad. Thinking about his lost sister? The city-folk adopted her out to new parents under a closed adoption, and he's never managed to locate her.

"Thanks, Bear," I say. "I couldn't have asked for a better birthday party."

A smile finally creeps onto his face. Billy glances at him and opens his mouth, but Ku gives him a sharp nudge and a significant look, and he rummages in his pocket instead.

"Here, cub," says Billy, holding something out. "Only just finished it. Took me twice as long as it shoulda because that cretin from PI got me the wrong wood. Far too hard. But it's done. Happy Birthday."

My cheeks get hot. Okay, I did notice they didn't give me nothing earlier, but I were trying not to think about it. I accept the little wooden ship he's offering—an old-fashioned sailing ship, with little masts and everything.

"Here," says Ku, handing me some folded paper. "This is a set of sails for it. You should be able to blow it around in your basin."

"Hey, this is totally *accurate*," I say, novelty being *far* more exciting in here than it normally would be. Wilhelm stares just as eagerly.

"Go on, go try it out," says Ku, waving a bony hand toward the sink.

"Just don't let the idiot capsize it, or you'll ruin the sails," Billy adds.

I jab Billy so hard my cardboard stick snaps in half—he and Ku laugh out loud. Bear grins too. So much for being discreet. My cheeks redden, making Wilhelm's lip tilt up slightly in that way that says he's thinking something involving the words *sweet*, *little*, and *cub*—but his eyes are happy. He ain't used to no one trying to stand up for him.

+

"Josh," says Wilhelm a few days later, "can I ask you something real important?"

I hide a smile. "Sure." Here comes some variation of "Dawn told me it's edmo pie and sticky toffee pudding for supper and sticky toffee pudding is a real, real favorite of mine, any chance you'd consider swapping yours for my pie?" He knows I'll probably just give it to him, but he still asks well in advance.

"Josh..." Wilhelm's turning a lollypop in his hands, but he ain't unwrapped it. Mebbe this is something more serious. I sit up in my bunk, paying attention.

He asks all in a rush, "Are we *friends*? Or just two guys they put in a cell together?"

136

My heart twists slightly. *Heck, Wilhelm, you have to ask? You find it so hard to believe anyone could like you?*

Then again, Ku and Billy don't. Nor Seb... Saint Des knows there are times when I wanna yell at Wilhelm to just *stop* cracking jokes and sucking and licking and pumping and apologizing... But I bet he could list a loada things I do that wind him up if he were ever mean enough to let rip at me. Even Dad and Uncle Z and Darryl and Harry did stuff that wound me up, big time, even if it's easy to forget now I'm not with them anymore and wish I were. Dad used to cross his legs when removing his gum boots, so they'd end up standing there by the door the wrong way around. Harry would put the mugs in the cupboard right way up instead of upside down. Uncle Z...heck, his *snoring*…

I drag my attention back to the present, 'cos Wilhelm's waiting real anxiously for my response.

"*Friends*, Wilhelm," I tell him. "Definitely friends."

He smiles, but then his face falls. Yeah, soon enough he's gonna be ignored by Ku and picked on by Billy.

Seeing his woebegone look gives me the resolve to say, "I'll come see you now and then, once I'm out, okay?"

He shakes his head disbelievingly. "You'll never walk back in *here*, just to see me."

"I *can* walk in here if I know they're gonna let me

walk out again and I will. Promise."

For a moment he smiles, real wide, but then pain drags his face down again. "I'm sorry I'm so...so thick and spineless. I know I...ain't much of a friend."

"Wilhelm, you're a great friend. You don't have to apologize for nothing. You come work for me when you get out, okay?"

"I'll...I'll definitely think about it." But the haunted look in his eyes tells me he's more likely to trot right back to Seb.

Darn, that guy's got his hooks into him real deep.

+

Wilhelm swallows the last spoonful of his bread and butter pudding. "That was good."

"Yeah." Contentedly, I eat another bite of mine. Fortunately Ku hates this dessert so much he always shoves his bowl across to Wilhelm without even asking for a trade.

"Say, Ku? If Billy can make wooden boats that float as good as the one he gave me, why are you folding paper ones all the time?" I ask.

"Something to do," he says.

"He's gotta nice remote-controlled boat back in the 'Vi," says Billy. "It were plastic, but I made a wooden hull for it instead. We know all the lakes and ponds and quiet streams around our neck of the woods where he can sail it or I can fish. With a beer..." His voice goes wistful. "On a sunny afternoon..."

"Ugh, be quiet. You know I can't stand it when you go on like that," snaps Ku, actually throwing a potato fry at his co-owner, then glancing at Wilhelm and me. "Quick, talk about something else before he can say nothing more."

I guess I know what those two spend most of their time doing, when they ain't in here.

I hide a smile. Then my eyes fix on the two guards that have just come into the hall from the door to the main prison—and the man between them. My breath catches in my throat and I flinch sideways, hiding behind Wilhelm's bulk. He twists, trying to see my face.

"What the heck, kid, you okay? You look like you saw a ghost."

Ku and Billy are peering at me too.

"Stop looking at me!" I hiss. "I don't want him to notice me." I've no sooner spoken than the awful truth hits me like a bullet. "*Misfire*, he's gonna see me soon enough, now he's here. That fresh fish they've just brought in? That's Jason Desmoines."

Their heads whip around, staring.

"Illegal-rex-farm,   probably-wants-to-kill-you, Jason?" queries Wilhelm.

"Yep." Actually...another man stands behind Jason, waiting as Jason argues with the guards about something. "Aw, *misfire, misfire, misfire*, that's Caleb, so

Jason knows. Make that *definitely* wants to kill me. *Both* of 'em, here! I'm *dead*!"

"No, you ain't, cub," says Ku firmly. "You're out in less'n two months, now, if you keep your nose clean. We've got your back. You simply can't be alone with either of 'em, ever."

Wilhelm turns to look at me again, his eyes wide and dismayed. Oh.

Billy bites at his thumb. "One bunk free in each cell. That won't do. Cub, you gotta shoot up there ahead of 'em and move your things to Hunter One."

"That means Wilhelm has to share with Jason and Caleb!" I protest.

"So? They don't know him from Adam, and he's bigger than either of 'em."

Wilhelm drops his gaze. Bigger, yeah, but I've a nasty feeling Jason's got a deal in common with Seb. "It's okay, Josh," Wilhelm says, in a low voice. "It's the only option."

Unless Ku and Billy are prepared to go in different cells for two months, but they ain't showing no sign of offering.

Wilhelm pushes to his feet. "I'll...I'll dash up there and move your things. That'll be...safer for you. I'll tell Hurst you're moving; I bet he'll be okay about it."

I hunch to put myself behind Ku's inadequate bulk as Wilhelm hurries toward Stairway Two. Near the base of Stairway One, Jason's waving his finger around, while Hurst stares at him like he can't decide whether to laugh or just taze him.

Caleb stands, hunched morosely, waiting. He's alive, at least. Despite what I told Harry, it did bother me, thinking he might be dead 'cos I let the rex out. Sure, he ran, and that was stupid. But I remember Dad telling me once: *You can't ever assume people will do the sensible thing, Josh, especially not when it really matters.*

No, you can't let fifty rex out and assume no one will die.

Hang on...

Caleb's missing his lower left arm.

"Oh heck. It don't get no better," I mutter.

"Now what?" asks Billy.

"I think I know what happened to Caleb's arm. And he probably thinks it were my fault. Mebbe were, a little."

If there were any question whether Caleb wants me dead just as much as Jason does, guess that settles it.

+

Wilhelm makes it back down to the hall before Jason and Caleb. "I simply told Hurst: 'The kid should go back in with Sekakuku and Billy,'" he announces. "Hurst just nodded. I didn't say your name in front of Jason."

"There's an unexpected show of intelligence," says

Billy.

"Oh, lay off," I snap then rest my forehead in my hand. "Sorry, Billy. But you don't have to be so mean all the time."

"Cub's gotta point," murmurs Sekakuku, earning an evil glare from Billy, which he ignores.

I close my eyes, stomach churning. Any moment, Jason and Caleb will come down here, and they can't miss me for long. Saint Des save me, I'm *locked* in this concrete and metal box with the pair of them, nowhere to run. If I had my rifle—or even my hunting knife—I'd feel more able to defend myself, but I ain't under no illusions about my abilities with my bare hands. Am I ever gonna see Darryl again?

"Hey." Wilhelm squeezes my shoulder with his strong hand. "It'll be okay, Josh. There're four of us and only two of them."

"One and a half," mutters Billy. "They're short-handed."

Ku laughs. Wilhelm just squeezes my shoulder again. My bad shoulder. Hey, doesn't hurt! I've just recovered from my last run-in with Jason in time for the next one.

Small mercies.

+

"Okay, they're coming down," murmurs Billy. "Looks like they're heading for the hatch to see if there's any lunch left."

I keep my head bowed.

"They've got their trays." Wilhelm takes over now they've passed us—I keep my face even further down. "They're looking around. For the hunter table, I guess."

We're all ducking our heads, now, as though Jason will be able to spot hunters just by looking at us, when we're sitting still as buzz-haired and orange-clad as everyone else. But it's gonna be a dangerous moment when he first sees me, and I guess none of us are keen to hasten it.

"Uh-oh, he's speaking to someone," mutters Wilhelm. "The guy's pointing our way. Yep, they're coming."

Every muscle in my body coils tightly. At least Jason won't have had time to sharpen his toothbrush yet.

"Is this the hunter table?" A familiar voice, with an edge to it, like Jason thinks we shoulda been rushing over to welcome him.

Ku gives up trying to play invisible, straightening and leaning back in a dignified manner befitting his position as eldest hunter present. "Yeah, this is the hunter table, and hunter rules apply. Mutual protection, no starting fights, no unnecessary mixing, no getting in with city-gangs, and *absolutely no fighting among ourselves*. You clear on those?"

Jason sneers, his gaze running over us. "Of course. You think I were born yester—?" His eyes settle on me, and rage explodes over his face. *"Wilson!"* He hurls his tray aside and hurtles forward. But Wilhelm's off his chair already, blocking his path, and a moment later Ku and Billy grip each of Jason's shoulders.

"What did we just say?" says Ku. "Hunter rules. No fighting among ourselves."

"You wanna sit at this table, you stick to those," growls Billy. "Otherwise, take a walk."

Jason spins around and starts to march away, but Caleb grabs his arm with his one hand, giving him a meaningful stare. Jason wrenches free of his brother's grip—but doesn't walk on. For long, long moments, he stands there with his back to us, shoulders rigid. Guess he's deciding whether trying to survive in a pack of two—or one and a half, as Billy would have it—is preferable to having to rub shoulders with me each day and not be allowed to kill me. Guess it's a tough decision.

Finally, he turns around again. His eyes burn as they drill into me, but he moves a couple of places along the table and sits. Caleb settles opposite him, and Jason starts helping himself to Caleb's food, since his is on the floor.

Guess he's gonna play nice.

Or pretend to.

Wilhelm comes to daily Mass with me in the morning, so Billy and Ku don't have to.

"You doing okay in there with the Desmoines brothers?" I ask him.

"Fine." But he's quiet enough I know that Jason and Caleb ain't being nice to him. Unfortunately it don't take long to look past Wilhelm's muscle and tattoos and realize he's more teddy bear than big bad bear.

"Did they tell you why they're here?"

He nods. "It was the rex farm. The idiots tried to keep it going, despite never catching all them rex you let out earlier in the year. So DAPdep found it in the end. Threw the book at them. Ten years."

I whistle. And Ku and Billy only got five for their little armed sorta-robbery. Just shows what happens when you mess with bureaucrats. Shame it weren't a few years longer still; Jason and Caleb would be in A-wing, but it has to be fifteen plus to get you in there.

When we come out of the chapel, an extra guard is waiting.

"Wilson, you have a visitor."

"I do?"

"Yeah, the usual one."

"I'll see you at lunch, Bear," I say, and follow the guard to the visitation room.

"Josh!" Father Ben rises to his feet as soon as I enter,

hurrying toward me, his face grave. Oh, he's here to warn me.

"He already arrived," I say tiredly.

"Jason?"

"And Caleb, yeah."

Father Ben shakes his head, gripping my shoulders until the bored guard drawls: "No Contact."

"Are you alright?" he asks, as we settle ourselves at the little table.

"Yeah." He looks so worried I try to sound confident as I say, "I get on real good with the other three hunters in here, and they've made it clear they ain't gonna let Jason or Caleb hurt me. I don't need to be alone with 'em, ever, and I'll be out in less than two months, Lord willing. So it ain't too bad."

He gives me a long searching look. "Really?"

I swallow, my attempt to put on a brave face wavering. "I..." I bite my lip. "Okay, I keep worrying I'm never gonna see Darryl again." The admission blurts out before I can stop it, propelled by the gnats that have filled my stomach since Jason arrived. "Or Harry. But...that's just fear talking. I'll be okay."

He nods then makes a face. "I'm sorry I couldn't make it sooner. I was right down in the south of my parish when I suddenly got bombarded with messages from Riley and Sandra saying those hunter friends of yours had called 'round in a panic, wanting someone to come see you and warn you that Jason was in the prison system. Obviously with the way they keep hunters only in particular prisons, there was a strong chance he'd end up in with you. I came as quickly as I could, but I had to celebrate a wedding first."

He sucks on his lower lip thoughtfully for a moment. "Don't get me wrong, I'm as worried as anyone else about Jason beating you up, but they seemed to think he might do something worse. Ten years in prison is bad enough, would he really want to up it to a life sentence?"

I shrug. I've been thinking about nothing else since yesterday. "I'm kinda afraid that's being too rational about it. The way Jason went for me when he saw me yesterday... Didn't have much to do with reason. Ten years is an awful long time for a guy Jason's age. He ain't the type to keep his nose clean and get early parole. He were already arguing with the guards. He does the full ten years and he'll be almost too old for active hunting when he gets out, have to become a camp-keeper, like as not, and he's a real proud weasel. He may not feel he's got much to lose."

"I didn't think there was any shame in being a camp-keeper."

"Not among sensible folk. Getting older ain't nothing to be ashamed of, and it takes all kinds to make a camp. But when folks are too full of pride, they get funny about things like that. He might prefer to soothe all that pride of his by at least killing me."

"Hmm." Father Ben nods. "Yeah, you're right about that. Not for nothing is pride considered the root of all other sins." He sighs. "You be very careful, you hear me?"

I laugh—shakily. "You bet."

+

A few days later, I'm already sitting at the hunter table with my new-old cellies when Jason and Caleb emerge from Hunter Two and come downstairs, Wilhelm trailing behind 'em. Once they've got their breakfast, Jason and Caleb settle a few seats along from us, ignoring all three of us the way they've been doing—and Wilhelm sits with 'em. He eats with his head bowed, not looking at us.

My stomach knots up. Seriously?

Billy's mouth twists in a sneer. "Look'it that, didn't take Jason long to get a leash on the dumb dog, did it?"

How awful are they being to Wilhelm that he's knuckling under to them already? Or can he just not help himself? They're now the closest people in his life, with the most power over him, so he desperately wants to please them. A teddy bear in a cageful of weasels ain't gonna last long. Poor Wilhelm.

"Right," says Ku, very firmly, "Wilhelm don't guard you no more, cub. He's with them, now. I guess it were too much to hope he wouldn't be."

"*He* ain't gonna hurt me," I say firmly. "But, yeah, I'd better stick with you and Billy."

+

It's wearing not being able to go nowhere without Ku and Billy. Fortunately—from my point of view—Jason likes to bend the no mixing rules even more than Seb did. During tier-time, he's often down in the hall, sitting at a table playing cards with the city-guys, Caleb slumped glumly beside him. Guess with a ten-year sentence he doesn't much care what the Elders think, though his camp are gonna be getting complaints all the same, if the Elders hear about it. Wilhelm stays up in Hunter Two, and I can go out and lean my elbows on the balcony and be more or less alone for a few minutes, without any risk of being surprised.

I keep hoping Wilhelm will come out and join me, but he don't. After a few days, I go to the cell doorway and look in. Can't go right in or I wouldn't see if Jason and Caleb were coming back.

"Hey, Bear," I call.

He's lying on his bunk—he still has a top one, whether because Jason wanted his brother sleeping beneath him rather than a stranger or because one-handed Caleb prefers a lower bunk, who knows—and his head jerks up from his chest, his eyes widening.

"Go away, kid," he whispers.

149

"Why? Am I gonna get you in trouble?"

His face crumples up in misery. "If they see. I'm sorry. I'm such a horrible friend. Why are you even talking to me?"

"Because you are my friend. And I'm real sorry you have to be in here with them."

"Weren't nothing else for it, kid. If I just do what Jason wants, it ain't no worse than Seb. Caleb ain't quite so bad."

"Is that supposed to make me feel better?"

"Forget it, kid." He shakes his head. "I should be by your side, watching out for you, not running at their heels like a licked dog. But that's what I am, I guess. I'm no friend. Worthless."

"Wilhelm, you're stuck in there with them to save my life!" Why can't I make him hear me? "If you have to avoid me and not sit with us to stay safe, then so be it. I ain't mad and we're still friends."

I glance over my shoulder. I need to check the hall, see where Jason and Caleb are...

He just keeps shaking his head. He don't even have a lollypop in his mouth. "I'm sorry," he whispers again. "I felt so brave and strong when they arrived. I really thought it was gonna be different, finally. But it ain't. I'm sorry. I should just be put down..."

"Wilhelm, *don't* talk like that..."

Ugh, instinct tells me it's been *far* too long since I

looked into the hall. I take a few quick steps to the rail. Darn, they're gone. They must be on their way back up. I dart back to the doorway. "We're still friends, Wilhelm, and you ain't worthless. Okay?"

But he just watches me flit away again, his eyes full of despair.

Safely back inside Hunter One, I prowl up and down the short length of cell, smacking my hands against the screens and the far wall, one, two, three. One, two, three. One, two, three.

"Cub, knock it off," growls Billy.

But I can't stop. Wilhelm's been getting so happy and confident since Seb left, but a few days with Jason and he's gone right back to how he was! It's so frustrating. And what about when I leave?

I finally stop pacing. "When they release me, can Wilhelm come in here with you two?"

"No," says Billy at once.

"Oh, come on! If Jason and Caleb hadn't turned up, he'd have been in here then!"

"Yeah, but luckily for Ku and me, those Desmoines boys did turn up."

I look at Ku. He purses his lips and sighs. "We'll think about it."

"No," says Billy. "The answer's no."

"We'll think about it, cub," says Ku.

"Will not," mutters Billy.

But it's the best answer I can get for now. I fetch my little craft project from my locker, climb onto my bunk, and sit cross-legged to work on it. I've got the mouse skeleton and fur, plus some cord and a few bits of wood, easily earned with the fancy writing business. I'm making it all into an angel singer, so I sing softly as I work, hunter ballads and hymns and psalms, sad ones 'cos I'm feeling sad and worried. I must be fairly tuneful 'cos neither of them object. Ku even hums along occasionally.

People put different numbers of silent chimes on these things, representing various things, even as many as ten, for the Ten Commandments. But I just put on three, carved with the symbols for faith, hope, and charity. I'll harvest a few feathers from each of my other angel singers to put on this one. And the mouse skeleton I'm gonna arrange artistically on the circle— with the trail sign for 'friend' above it.

+

Someone must've told Jason I visited Wilhelm, because Jason's keeping Wilhelm on a real tight leash now, taking him down to the hall with him and not leaving him alone for a second. It makes me so mad.

Wilhelm never even seems to have a lollypop anymore. Is Jason taking 'em? Since a lollypop takes a long time to eat, giving Jason far too much opportunity to swipe it, I get a selection of Wilhelm's favorite wrapped candies from the store instead and start slipping him one as we pass each other, whenever I can do it without Jason seeing.

Despite my candy smuggling offensive, Wilhelm carries on staring at me from a distance with his big, miserable eyes, like he just can't believe I can forgive him for going over to the enemy, as he clearly sees it. I was originally making the angel singer for Wilhelm's birthday in late November but, once it's finished, I get Ku and Billy to keep guard for me during a mealtime when Hunter Two is empty, and I slip in and hang it inside Wilhelm's locker. He should see it before Jason, and he can hide it if he thinks he needs to.

Billy rolls his eyes and grumbles as we hurry down to get in the food line afterwards, but I ignore him.

The next time I see Wilhelm, he sneaks me a smile. When Jason and Caleb ain't looking, of course. And a few days later, he comes up behind me and slips something into *my* hand. When I get back to Hunter One I take a look. It's a pebble from the yard, with a cursive-style *j* carved into it and inked. I put it carefully on the window ledge, my stomach unknotting a little for the first time since Jason arrived.

He's finally getting the message. *Yeah, Wilhelm, still friends. And Jason can't do nothing about that.*

+

"Bet that's an H, is it?" asks Ku, as I examine the

latest rock Wilhelm's slipped me.

"Yep." I've survived more than two weeks of Jason's presence now, and the nasty weasel remains oblivious to the fact that Wilhelm and I are defying him with our little game—I think. Once, I were afraid Caleb mighta seen me make the pass, but Jason don't seem to know, so mebbe he didn't.

I add the pebble to the other three on the window ledge: *j o s h.*

"One month, and you'll be out," says Ku. "I guess he'll manage a U and an A in that time."

"Can he share with you guys, then?"

"No," says Billy.

"We're still thinking about it," says Ku.

+

One month. I can hardly bear to let myself imagine it, as I take an alone moment here on the balcony outside Hunter One, in case it don't happen. That's the earliest possible date, after all. My case will go before the parole board in a week or two. But I've had no misdemeanors, and they always seemed to understand that my phobia was a genuine issue and not me making trouble. Totally clean record. Surely they'll let me out?

"Josh?" Wilhelm sounds nervous as he peeps out of Hunter Two. "Can I talk to you for a minute?"

"Sure." Jason and Caleb are below in the hall, so I follow him into the cell. "I can't stay in here for long,

154

though."

"I know. Jason's got some real important card game going, though."

"Ah. Are you okay?" He don't look it. "I really miss sharing with you, y'know. Ku and Billy are nice enough to me, but they just do their own thing. Don't wanna play ball and stuff. Fortunately I can use the bars more, now, so I ain't going nuts, but we had fun together, didn't we?"

"Yeah...yeah, I...I really miss all that too," he mumbles, his eyes wide and darting here and there, not making eye contact.

"Bear? You okay? Are they *real* awful to you?"

"Don't worry about me, kid," he whispers. "I'm...I'm a coward, and cowards are good at surviving."

"I dunno if you are, Bear," I say. "One thing you are is real sensitive. You don't like to disappoint people. Even nasty people who don't deserve nothing from you."

He hangs his head as though he can't look at me. "Ah, kid, you're so *nice*. I'm a coward, okay? That's all I am."

"You can say *that* again. Well done, doggie." The sneering voice speaks from the doorway and I spin around, my heart rate kicking up.

Jason.

No hint of surprise on Wilhelm's miserable face before I turned... Darn, this is a trap. He ain't gonna help me. But Ku and Billy are just next door...

I open my mouth to yell, but Jason's foot slams into my stomach, smacking me back into the lockers and driving all the breath from my lungs.

Josh, get out *of here!*

Gasping, helplessly winded, I try to dodge him, staggering, aiming for the doorway, but he grabs me by the collar, dragging me sideways, then sweeps my legs out from under me and rams my head into the toilet.

I hold my breath as my face goes under, though I'm already desperate for oxygen after that stomach blow, then his knee drives into my belly, expelling what little air remains. My stupid body tries to drag in a breath and draws in water. I manage to swallow most of it, but some goes into my lungs, burning and triggering a spasm of coughing that lets more water in.

Choking, I struggle, trying to get my knees under me, trying to claw, to hit, to grab at Jason...*air!*...but with my shoulders wedged into the toilet bowl, I can't...*air, please!*...reach back to him, can't grab *anything.* Something...his knee?...is in between my...*O God, air, please?*...shoulder blades, his full body weight holding me down...

He ain't planning to let me up any time soon.

The knowledge hammers panic and adrenalin

156

through my system. I throw my body around with all my strength, pushing with my legs, trying to grip the smooth floor enough with my knees to get the leverage to draw back despite his weight. One ear comes out of the water, assaulted by cool air and crisp, clear sounds: splashing and sloshing and soft grunting from Jason as he holds me down and Wilhelm's distraught, "...you *swore* you were only gonna..."

My knee slips and my ear plunges under the water again. My body tries another breath of water and most of it goes into my lungs. My strength is draining away.

I've gotta...gotta fight... Gotta...

But my body slumps limply, refusing to obey. I can't breathe. I can't live.

Darryl, Harry, I'm so sorry...

Fight, Josh!

Is that you, Saint Des?

Guess there's only one way I can fight now.

Jesus, I trust in you. Jesus, I trust in you... The familiar words of the chaplet fill my mind as the panic and pain give way to an eerie sense of peace. Blackness starts to spiral in around me.

The force pressing on my dimly-remembered back suddenly lifts, and my body weight drags me sideways. My head smacks the industrial linoleum beside the toilet, and my chest heaves convulsively. Somehow I manage to jerk over onto my side to help clear my lungs as I spew and vomit up water.

Air! My chest burns as I suck it in, but it feels so good. A hint of strength floods my body with every breath, though I remain slumped, each limb weighing the same as a juvenile rex.

I finally manage to look up.

Jason's just dragging himself free from Wilhelm's bear hug, a smear of blood around his mouth. Wilhelm backs away, placing himself between me and Jason, clutching his arm—I guess Jason bit him.

"Help!" Wilhelm's bellowing in his deep voice, "Help! Murder! Guards! Help!"

How long has he been shouting? I don't even know. *Air, air, thank you God!*

"*You*—" Jason cuts himself off as he launches himself at Wilhelm full tilt, ramming him backward. Wilhelm's head smacks into the metal door frame, and his eyes roll up. He crumples to the ground. *No...!*

Face twisted with rage, Jason stamps on Wilhelm's head with manic force, immediately raising his foot again.

Heck, Wilhelm's down but Jason ain't stopping!

My arms as limp as a dead octopus's tentacles, I grope for something, anything, I can chuck at Jason. My throw surely makes a new record for feebleness, but the sodden toilet roll squelches wonderfully as it hits the back of Jason's neck, making him flinch and bat it away.

And spin around, his eyes skewering me. *Uh-oh.*

I make a pathetic attempt to get up, my chest still heaving uncontrollably, my legs no more willing to report for duty than my arms. The next moment Jason's on top of me, his knees on my chest, his hands around my throat, and air is just a fond memory again.

No! No...

I struggle, the final twitchings of a landed fish, as Jason's bared teeth, his triumphant sneer, fill my vision. But a movement over his shoulder draws my gaze. For a split second my eyes focus on the probes of Hurst's taze-gun as they sail through the air toward Jason's back—then everything explodes in pain...

...and darkness.

+

"Deeper," I tell Darryl. "Think of the size of an allo's chest. The depth. They rumble."

Again I imitate an allosaur's territorial warning call—or a 'back off, my patch' as I'm used to calling it—and she tries again.

"Better. You sound more like a rex, though. Whatever the city-folk think, a roar is not a roar is not a roar. Try and listen to the complexities of it. Listen, I'll do them both."

She listens intently as I roar again, twice.

"Which was the allo?" I ask.

"The first?"

"Yep. Now, concentrate on how you knew, and try to

imitate it."

She roars again—much better this time.

Harry's tousled head pops up through the open hatch, his face tense and annoyed. "What the heck kinda 'saur is that?" he demands. "A let's-wake-Harry-o-saur?"

I laugh at his indignation and so does Darryl. "It's seven o'clock, Harry," I say. "Sun's well up. Ain't getting no sympathy from me."

When I open my eyes the ceiling above me is a lighter grey than that of Psych Ward and smoother. I stare at it for a while. Why do my chest and neck and throat hurt so much? Too much roaring?

Full consciousness finally comes in a rush, and I look around quickly. Medical, not Psych Ward. I glance at my wrist and wish I hadn't. The handcuff is there, a serious challenge even to my much-improved phobia.

Quickly, I grab the blanket and pull it sideways, flop it over the side of the bed, covering the handcuffs. It's easier if I can't see it. I've learned a trick or two.

One of the prison nurses is already approaching the bed.

"Awake?" She smiles at me. "How do you feel?"

My mind is still playing catch-up... "Wilhelm! How is he?"

Her face sobers. "Fenn was transferred to Exception Central Hospital. He's been placed in an induced coma as a precaution, just while they run some tests. But the prison doctor's confident it's just a concussion, nothing he won't make a good recovery from. No skull fracture or obvious evidence of more serious brain injury."

I bite my lip. Induced coma? Still, if it's just precautionary...

"Relax, Wilson," says the nurse. "Doctor Green has worked here for fifteen years, and I can assure you that he has *very* extensive experience with head injuries."

I bet.

"Fenn may be in the hospital for a while — concussion *is* more serious than the movies like to make out. But he'll be back, don't you worry."

"Within a month?" I ask.

Her eyebrows rise. "I imagine he'll at least be back here in Medical by then, but that's really not a prediction I'm qualified to make. Now, how are *you* feeling?"

"Chest hurts some when I breathe." I raise a hand to my neck, then regret it. "And, uh, bruises here. I think I'm okay. Can I go back to Gen Pop?" *Can you uncuff me, please?*

"Probably, once the doc's checked you over."

Thank you, God, thank you, Saint Des!

+

"Cub! You okay?" Even creaky Ku surges to his feet at the sight of me. Billy jumps up too as the cell door clanks and clicks closed behind me.

"Yeah." I nod. "I've gotta go to Medical every day for a check-up until the doc's happy I ain't gonna come down with pneumonia or some'at like that." After inhaling and swallowing the contents of Hunter Two's watery city-toilet—I am really trying not to think about that. "But I guess they know me well enough by now to figure that trying to keep me *there* for observation might be, er, counterproductive."

Even the short walk from Medical has tired me—that and the interview with the Prison Investigation Officer where I had to give my version of what the heck happened yesterday—and I sink onto the chair Billy vacated, feeling a little light-headed. Mebbe I should just lie down awhile.

"*Misfire*, cub, that musta been a close one. When they carted you outta there unconscious..."

"I got tazed, along with Jason. But yeah." I shiver. "It were a close one."

Click. Clank. We all look around in surprise as the door slides open again. Two different guards enter. Hurst and the no longer quite-so-greenhorn Poulter.

"Wilson?" Hurst sounds uncomfortable.

"Yeah?" Unease prickles down my spine at his tone.

"Central Hospital have been in touch with the Warden. It seems, despite what was initially believed, that...well, that Fenn isn't going to make it."

His words punch me full in the stomach. "*What?*"

"Fenn's asked to see you. Warden's sorted out the paperwork. We're to take you there now—if you want to go."

I stare at him, my insides buzzing emptily. *Ain't gonna make it?* What happened to *just a concussion?*

"Do you wish to make use of the compassionate furlough?"

The what? "I wanna see him, yeah!"

I push to my feet, grabbing my locker door half for balance and half 'cos I wanna open it. I snatch up the handful of lollypops I've got leftover from my time sharing with Wilhelm, plus the remaining candy I've been slipping to him, and cram it all into my pockets. I guess he'll be all hooked up on life support and won't be able to touch any of it—but I ain't got nothing else to take him.

I grab the lurid orange jacket that's been issued for yard-time now the weather's turning colder and slip into it.

"Hang on, hang on," says Ku, his gaze flicking between me and Hurst as he flaps his lean hand in a restraining gesture. "Central Hospital? You're taking him outside the prison?"

"That's right," says Hurst.

"Come on, cub, this ain't a good idea."

"One month," says Billy, "and you'll be outta here for good. It ain't worth risking this."

I pause, staring at them as it sinks in. *Outside the prison.* Oh, Saint Des help me, will I be able to keep it together?

"I've gotta go see him."

"You don't gotta," says Ku. "How'd you even get caught by Jason like that, anyway? It were Wilhelm, weren't it?"

I don't reply.

"Typical," snaps Billy. "You don't owe him nothing, cub. Just stay here."

"I'm going." I turn toward the guards.

"Wait up." Ku fishes in his locker, turns, and pulls a woolly hat down over my head. "Take this."

"It's only October—"

"You can wear it like this..." He folds the turn-up down, so it covers my eyes.

"*Hey—*"

I try to yank it off, but Billy stops me, folding the hat up again to clear my vision. "Ku's right. Take the hat, cub. Just remember, if you run, they will shoot you, and out there, it won't be with a taze-gun."

"One more month, and you get to live the rest of your life," says Ku. "Don't forget it, cub. Keep it together."

"I plan to." I say it as confidently as I can, turning toward the door.

"Make sure you look surprised when he blurts out

that big *secret* of his," smirks Billy.

"I ain't gonna act surprised *at all*," I say firmly.

"Yeah," says Ku, "that's a much nicer way to deal with it."

I follow the guards through the prison. Finally, we reach a lobby I should probably remember from when I arrived but don't. Heck, I were out of it. Hurst accepts something from the guy behind the grilled-off desk and approaches me.

Shackles. That's what he's holding. The two sets of cuffs, the belt for the waist, the short chains... I stare at them, my stomach turning over. *No, no, no.*

"Have I gotta wear those?"

Hurst gives me a sympathetic look. "If you go out that door to the transport vehicle, you wear them. Or we can take you back to your cell. Those are the only two choices."

I bite my lip. If I freak out and try to run, I'll be dead on a slab in the morgue... No. I barely could run in those things. Surely I wouldn't get far enough for them to feel they needed to shoot me? I'd have to find some way to get 'em off, and that would require so much cooperation from my will I couldn't possibly do it by *accident*, in the grip of some phobic fit, right? Surely I can keep it together long enough to get in and out of a car a few times? I really am so much better now. Hard to believe, but those shackles will keep me safe.

"Okay."

But when Hurst steps toward me, I jink backward without meaning to.

Heck, Josh! You gotta let him put 'em on you!

"You want to just go back to your cell, Wilson?" suggests Hurst.

I *could* go back to my cell. No shackles... No. Wilhelm's lying in that hospital bed, hoping to see a friendly face before he—

I hold out my wrists. "Put 'em on."

+

The shackles are in place, hobbling me to a shuffling walk, making panic fizz through my gut. Hurst and Poulter have signed something and swapped their tazeguns for handguns and now Poulter is opening that door. When I glimpse the city skyline, I almost imagine I can see the city-fence, though it's probably too far away. Quickly, I try to raise my hands, but I'm shackled now, so I can't.

"Wait! Could you...put the hat down?" My voice goes small with embarrassment.

Hurst does so. Without laughing at me. Probably doesn't want to shoot me any more than I wanna be shot.

They walk me outside, each holding an arm tightly, and fold me carefully into the mini-van. It smells of feet more than anything, Saint Des knows why. I try to keep breathing slow and steady as the vehicle purrs along, try to simply focus on the motion as we stop and turn and slow and accelerate.

It obviously ain't far, because soon we've pulled to a halt, the engine switches off, and they're getting me out again. City-smells assault my nose, choking fumes and wafting food scents and teeming humanity. I keep my eyes tight closed, even behind my hat-blindfold, and let them guide me.

The soft, tell-tale sound of automatic doors, and we're inside a building, no more wind on my cheeks. Cleaning products and medical smells sear my nostrils now. Voices buzz and echo, machines beep, carts rumble. We go on a little further, then Hurst's voice says, "I'm going to fold the hat up again now, okay?"

I nod, so he does. Yep, we're in a hospital. A kid sitting on a woman's lap in a waiting area nearby stares hard at me, at my shackles and orange—until the mother flicks me an anxious look and sets about distracting her offspring. 'Cos all cons are vicious animals that will run mad if stared at, sure. Would she be less scared of me if I were dressed like a hunter—or more? Poulter's voice echoes in my head: *It's a baby's hand. They've eaten it!*

Hurst's getting a room number from the nurse. We head into an elevator—*ugh*—and along corridors. Finally we're entering a quiet ward, and a nurse behind a desk is nodding and pointing across the hallway. "Mr. Fenn is in there."

This don't look like an ICU in the movies. Weird.

"Poulter, stay here with Wilson," says Hurst. "I need to check the room over before we can let him in there." He disappears inside.

I wait, tensely.

Poulter waits—tensely. Eventually, he relaxes enough to ask, "Did you really get bit by a rex?"

"Yeah."

"And you really cut its throat?"

"No, I lay in the snow and bled until someone came and helped me get up."

He still shoots me a wide-eyed look. Like a lot of young city-guys, he makes me feel way older than him—though I almost certainly ain't.

He opens his mouth then shoots a sheepish look at the room doorway and closes it again. Yeah, finally remembered that I might not feel like chit-chat right now.

Hurst's speaking inside the room... "...warden said he's trying to contact Father Timaru, but it's his day off so he hasn't managed it yet. But there's a hospital chaplain here."

Wilhelm's voice, faint and slightly petulant. "...I don't want the chaplain. I already spent ages speaking to that Prison Investigation guy. I wanna see *Wilson*..."

"He's here. I'll send him in."

Hurst appears, beckoning to me. When I approach, he removes the shackles just from my wrists, securing the empty cuffs through the belt to keep them tidy.

"Okay, you can go in. We'll be out here. You can, er, stay as long as you like."

I nod, my mouth dry. Once I've shuffled past him, he closes the door behind me. No surprise, since I see at a glance that the sturdy room window is closed and presumably locked, and we're high up anyway, quite apart from my shackled legs. There's a sickly-looking plant on the window ledge—good. Then my gaze focuses on the bed.

Wilhelm's lying there, his face somewhat bruised down each side, an IV running into one wrist and a sensor to his forefinger, but other than that he looks fine. No sinister machines keeping him alive. The tell-tale metal ring of a cuff shows at the foot of the bed, obviously secured to his ankle.

I can't stop my heart from lifting a little. Has the diagnosis got garbled? Is it not so bad?

One look at his face as his eyes shift to mine and I know nothing's got garbled, because the fear and despair that stare back at me...

"Hey, Bear." I drag the chair into position beside the bed, hobbling awkwardly in the leg shackles, then sit down and grab his hand. "How...how are you?"

"Didn't they tell you?"

"Yeah, they...they told me but—I'd be real happy to hear something different."

He starts to shake his head then aborts the movement, a flicker of terror crossing his face. "It's bad, Josh, it's..." He breaks off, chewing his lip, then takes a deep breath. "Okay, so, they thought it was just a concussion, thought this thick skull of mine had kept me safe." He pauses, his gaze wandering around the room for a moment, like he's lost his thread. I guess whatever else is wrong, he has a concussion too.

"Uh"—he catches his thread again—"they put me in some coma thing and did some scans just to make sure. And, uh...they found this place in my brain where a weak spot had, kinda, *almost* ruptured. There's a bubble of blood bulging out of a vein or art-ry or some'at. Just one layer of mem...er...memb..."

"Membrane?"

"Yeah, that. Just one single layer, ever so thin, still holding. And it's just a matter of time and it's gonna pop and when it does"—his voice shakes—"that's gonna be it."

"But...can't they get in there and *fix* it?" That's what they do, ain't it, in these amazing city-hospitals?

"Often," he whispers. "But not this. Wrong place, too thin. It would break before they got to it, no point even trying, that's what they say. So they, er..." He loses his thread again, blinks, then focuses on me again. "So, uh, they woke me up. Normally they'd have left me longer, or something, to heal, but they woke me up in case" —he swallows hard— "in case there were anything I wanted to take care of, y'know? Given me something for the head pain and to unscramble me as much as possible. And...and that's it. They sent some fella in to help me write a...a will" —his voice shakes— "so I done that, leastways."

He opens his mouth like he's gonna say something else then looks confused for a moment. Finally, he shoots me a shy glance. "Oh, uh, he said I had real nice handwriting!"

I manage a smile. "You do." I swallow. "Did they say, er, how long...?"

"They *said* maximum twenty-four hours. But the way they're acting..." He gulps.

You can stay as long as you like, Hurst told me. Yeah, *they* ain't been told no 'twenty-four hours,' have they? A few hours, more like.

"There ain't no rush for me to get back to the prison, by the sound of it," I simply say. "So I ain't going nowhere." I squeeze his hand, and he grips back tightly. "But, uh, you wanna see the chaplain?"

He almost shakes his head again but stops, clearly scared of popping that bubble. "No. I wanna...I wanna talk to you, kid. I'm, I'm real sorry about" —his face goes vague—"was it yesterday? Y'know, Jason..."

"It's okay, Bear, forget it. You saved me, remember? You were real brave, standing up to Jason like that."

"It was my fault you needed saving."

"Yeah, but, I'm real sorry what it's cost you."

"Me too, kid," he whispers.

"Do you regret—" I bite off the words before I can finish. How can I ask him that? "Uh, are you sure you wouldn't like to see the chaplain?"

"No. There's something I...something I need to tell you."

His face is so drawn and strained.

"Wilhelm, it's alright. I know you weren't driving the 'Vi that night, okay? Seb was. You wanted him to stop, but he wouldn't, and then he made you take all the blame."

His eyes widen. "How do you—?"

"Ku and Billy and anyone who's ever spent half a day with you and Seb know that, Wilhelm. Shame a jury didn't."

His face falls. "Guess it doesn't really matter now, does it?"

"If it's important to you that someone knows, then it does."

"Yeah." He stares at me for a long time, fear and unease and longing and dread flitting across his face, like he's wrestling with some temptation. Finally he closes his eyes for a moment, with a long sigh. "Kid, that wasn't what I need to tell you."

"It weren't?"

"No. I'm just so scared that once I tell you" —his voice goes almost inaudible—"you'll leave."

"Leave?" I tighten my grip on his hand. "I ain't gonna *leave*, Wilhelm. You're my friend."

He gives another huge sigh, so much fear in his gaze. "You *will*. But...I think I gotta anyway. It's just eating at me, kid."

"Okay. Whatever it is, you can tell me. I won't go nowhere."

He almost shakes his head, stops himself again, face slumping in despair. "Okay, kid. I'm gonna tell it from the beginning 'cos I don't think I can say it straight. So, uh, Seb's fairly good with money, right? Except that he's like Jason, too fond of gambling. He'd do well for himself, financially, even for a year or two at a time, no gambling, then he'll fall off the wagon and get himself into real trouble. That's how he came to sell twenty-five percent of his 'Vi to me. He'd run up a loada debts he needed to pay off quick. Y'know how shameful guys find it to hafta sell part of their 'Vi. He didn't like it."

He trails off for a minute, frowning and blinking. I wait patiently. Where's he going with this?

"Anyway, uh, a little over a year ago, he got himself in deep again. He shoulda just sold another share in the

'Vi, like mine. He'd still have had fifty percent, still have been the clear 'Vi-boss. But he were too ashamed. And probably didn't want to risk getting someone more uppity than me."

He pauses again, not looking confused this time, just resting or gathering his thoughts.

"Anyway, he started taking us to these city-joints, and he'd leave me in the bar to have a drink or a milkshake and he'd disappear into these back rooms to *talk to people*. Didn't take me long to figure out that he were looking for a well-paid job and not the kind they advertise on notice boards—jobs those back-room crooks might just help you find if they think you're up to it."

Wilhelm's eyes slide away from mine, then jerk back, filled with remembered desperation. "I *tried* to talk him out of it, Josh, tried to get him to sell a share, even offered to sell five percent of mine so it could be twenty-twenty-sixty in his favor, so we could just go on hunting, everything more or less above board, but he just wouldn't listen! He weren't giving up no more of his 'Vi, and he didn't care what he had to do to keep it."

A tiny worm of disquiet wriggles in my belly.

"Then one night he headed back to the 'Vi all cock-a-hoop, and I knew he'd found something. When we were alone he told me, he told me it all. This city-guy them crooks had put him in touch with was paying him—us—whichever—to snatch some farmer and kill him. It had to look like an accident. An animal attack."

I draw in a sharp breath—*no, no, no!*—but Wilhelm won't look at me.

"I tried to talk him out of it. I tried and tried. He wouldn't listen. And he'd told me everything, Josh!" He looks at me now, his eyes pleading before slumping back into shame. "Every last *misfiring* detail. *Who, what, how much...* You wanna know when I really knew what Seb was? It were then, when I realized that I knew perfectly well he'd never let me walk away with that info in my head. That he'd kill me first. That he'd told me it all deliberately, just so I couldn't back out."

I close my eyes, unable to bear the misery in his eyes. "So you went along with it?"

Of course he did. He went along with luring me into that cell for Jason and the stakes weren't anything like as high—not for him.

"Yes," whispers Wilhelm. "We made a plan. We headed out to the farm. We snatched the guy easily enough. Farmers' fences aren't hard to get around, and Seb knew exactly how to do it. We were gonna take him far into the wilds, just cut him and chuck him out, then keep watch until there was nothing left. No one would ever know—so Seb kept telling me."

I wrap my arms around myself, my stomach churning. *Oh Darryl, Harry, your dad...*

"I didn't wanna," says Wilhelm. "I never wanted to do something less in my life. But I realized something. This farmer guy we'd snatched, I'd heard his name before. When I was waiting in all them bars for Seb, I was drinking with some country-fella one evening. Country-guys like that often like to buy hunters drinks, hang out with us in front of the city-folks, makes 'em feel like real hard men, have you noticed?"

I bite my lip, reeling too badly to answer.

A pause to collect his thoughts and he hurries on. "Uh...yeah, this country-guy was going on about this farmer. How much he'd like to lay his hands on him, see him dead. And he lived in the same area. I told Seb about it. Suggested we sell the farmer to this guy, get paid twice and keep our hands cleaner. Seb liked the idea of getting paid twice, I can tell you. But he was real wary about not seeing the job through. He didn't want trouble with them city in-ter-mee-drees who'd set him up with the city-guy..."

He trails off, staring around the room like he's totally lost his chain of thought. After a moment, he murmurs, "I'm real thirsty."

My hands shaking, I pick up the glass of water from the bedside table and hand it to him. He sips for a while. Finally, the confusion clears from his face. His eyes dart to me, wide and fearful. I take the glass back and wait.

"So...um..." He speaks in a whisper. "So Seb met this country-guy a few times, hashed out a deal, and when he were convinced enough that the country-guy had meant what he said, we handed the farmer over and took the money. And off we went. And a few days later, Seb were driving, far too late and slightly drunk, and he hit that poor woman's car. And wouldn't stop. And that were that."

He stops, breathing shakily. "So that's it, Josh. That's why you're in jail. 'Cos of me. This is what you've been so sweet and kind to all these months. A murderer. As good as. And I'm sorry. I'm *so, so* sorry, but it don't fix nothing."

I wrap my arms around myself again to try to still their trembling.

"Wilhelm, how could you?" I whisper. "He even had the same name as you, near enough..."

His face crumples, a tear running down his cheek, but he doesn't seem able to answer. I struggle to think, trying to put aside my shock and ask the questions I need to ask. "So..." I have to pause and moisten my lips. "So, uh, you never actually saw William Franklyn dead?"

He almost shakes his head and stops himself again. "No. He were tranked but alive when we handed him over. I wanted to believe that since the country-guy were sober then, unlike in the bar, mebbe he wouldn't actually kill him after all. But Seb were satisfied he meant it and the farmer's still missing, so...so I guess he did it." Wilhelm's eyes drop from mine again, filled with shame.

"Wilhelm," I say, trying to keep my voice steady. "Thank you for telling me. It will mean a lot to Darryl and Harry even to know this much. Will you...will you please tell me the names?"

He moistens his own lips, taking a moment to overcome his now pointless instinct to keep silent. "Yeah," he whispers "Yeah, I will."

And he does. The first name confuses me, until I figure out who it must be. The second... I put my face in my hands.

Oh Darryl, oh Harry, I'm so sorry...

Misery covers his face when I look up again. "You can go," he whispers. "I can't ask you to stay. Why would you? O God, Josh, I'm so sorry! I'm *so sorry...*" He's weeping, long choked sobs as he tries to keep control, to not get in a state, to not burst his head.

I close my eyes, bury my face back in my hands, almost too confused to think straight.

Wilhelm, how could you?

I'm a coward, and cowards are good at surviving. Huh, and he finally tried not being a coward yesterday and now he's dying... That stinks.

To truly love someone, we must love them as they are,

not as we would like them to be. That is how God loves each one of us.

He is who he is. He's done what he's done. He's sorry. Real sorry. Guess all those nightmares weren't just about the accident, after all...

I look up at last. Tears are still running down his face. I reach out, unclench his hand from the blankets, and slip my fingers back into his grasp instead.

He stares, bewildered.

"Wilhelm, I forgive you."

"*Forgive* me?"

"Yeah. Hunter-born, remember? Saint Des likes forgiveness."

He says nothing, either too shocked or struck by another wave of concussion confusion. How long does he have?

"Wilhelm?"

"Yeah?"

"Will you do something for me?"

"What?"

"See the chaplain. Get your soul scrubbed clean of all this before it's too late."

"God doesn't want *me*, Josh." Wilhelm's deep voice sounds small, like a lost child. "Free will, like you said. I *coulda* said no."

"Of course he wants you. *Anything* we do wrong we *coulda* said no to. Please let me get the chaplain?"

A mulish look covers his face. He's just afraid to hope he could really be forgiven, isn't he? In case it's offered and then snatched away, like Seb taunting him with a sugary treat.

"Wilhelm, I know Darryl and Harry would want you to see the chaplain. I'm sure they'd forgive you, if you did."

Surely they'd forgive him anyway, but I don't reckon there's time for subtlety.

He frowns. "You can't know that."

"I can. They're like-family to me. You see the chaplain, and I will pledge you their forgiveness with complete confidence."

He stares at me for a while, wide-eyed. The thought of *their* forgiveness obviously means a lot to him. Heck, I hope they're okay with this. But of course they will be. What else would they do?

Finally, he swallows. And says in a tiny voice, "'Kay."

+

While we wait for the chaplain to arrive, Wilhelm stares dazedly out the window, until I remember something and dig in my pockets.

"Wilhelm, here. Are you allowed to eat?" Can't imagine why not, considering.

His eyes brighten at the sight of the lollypops. "Hey, Josh, you're a" —his face crumples then firms—

"well, not quite a lifesaver, but...thanks."

He's about to rip the wrapper off one when there's a tap at the door, and Father Timaru looks in. "Wilhelm, Joshua, hello. I came as soon as I heard. They said you asked for the hospital chaplain to be fetched a moment ago. Are you happy with me or would you rather wait for him?"

I glance at Wilhelm, who looks horrified at the thought of telling all this to someone he knows, even slightly. But he might not have long, and I bet Father Timaru's used to coaxing real bad stuff out of people and saying the best thing in response.

"I'll leave you with Father Timaru, Wilhelm." Panic covers his face as I rise to my feet. "I'll just be outside," I add quickly. "I'll come back in when he's done, I *promise.*" I squeeze his hand and hobble-shuffle across the room. Father Timaru gives me a searching look as he passes, so I must look like I've been knocked over the head with a two by four. I feel like it.

I close the door behind me and glance around the ward's reception area. Hurst and Poulter sit in some chairs opposite, sipping coffee, though Hurst's putting his down quick and sitting up alertly at the sight of me. I move over to them, nice and steady and slow—not that it's possible to do anything else, wearing these...*no, don't think about them, Josh.*

"Wilhelm's seeing Father Timaru. I promised I'd go

back in, after."

Hurst nods. "Okay. You can sit down and wait. Poulter, why don't you go grab him a coffee? Kid looks like death warmed over."

Feel like that, too. Not so far off, considering what happened yesterday.

I sink down into one of the fancy seats, barely holding back a real old guy kinda sigh. I ain't sat on a soft padded seat for *months*. Everything's hard plastic at the prison.

No, don't think about the prison, Josh...

+

Despite everything—my seething mind and whirling emotions and a real nice cuppa non-prison coffee—I'm dozing exhaustedly when the click of the room door jerks me awake. The clock on the wall shows that it's been forty-five minutes. Father Timaru beckons to me, so I get up and shuffle back inside.

Wilhelm's eyes light up at the sight of me. Yep, he really thought I'd high-tail it outta here, didn't he?

"Josh?" He speaks timidly.

I sit again and take his hand. "How'd it go?"

He smiles—also timidly. "Well, I told him everything and he did a bunch of stuff, lots of sacra-thingies. Even baptized me, 'cos I ain't sure I ever were. Dunno why my parents woulda done it. I never heard nothing about God till I became a hunter."

Oh yeah, city-born. Some city-folk are religious, of course, but a lot ain't.

"And, y'know, that's real good" —his eyes brighten again—"'cos he said if I really weren't baptized 'til now, that means I don't have to do no purgatory, can you imagine? I just go straight up!"

"Really?" I smile, my chilly insides warming a little. "That's great, Bear."

"Ain't it? Anyway"—Wilhelm shoots a glance at Father Timaru, who's sat back down on the other side of the bed—"y'can relax, Raptor Boy, 'cos he says I'm all cleaned up and"—his face crumples—"*ready to go.*"

I squeeze his hand. "I'm real sorry you're going, Bear, but I'm real glad you're right with God."

"Me too, kid." His brows draw down and he speaks warily. "They had a...a *nice* dad, like you did, and I...took him away from them. D'you...d'you really think they could ever forgive me?"

I nod. "They do. I'm telling you so, right now, on their behalf, okay? God forgives you. I forgive you. Darryl and Harry Franklyn forgive you."

He meets my steady gaze for a while. "Okay," he whispers at last, smiling like he finally believes it. *Thank you, Saint Des!*

After a while, he unwraps a lollypop and sticks it in his mouth, then offers one to me and Father Timaru. It'll make him happy if I accept, so I do, and so does Father.

We sit and suck in silence for a while. Deathwatch with lollypops. Well, it is Bear.

"D'you want the answer?" he says suddenly.

"Huh?"

"*Do I regret it?*"

Heat floods my face. "I shoulda never asked that, Bear. What the heck are you supposed to say?"

"The truth, mebbe." He sucks fiercely for a moment. "I've been thinking about it since you said it. And I don't wanna die, don't get me wrong, so my first thought was *heck, yeah*. I'm crapping myself right now. If someone walked in here and said they had a way to save me, but I had to do something bad, *misfire*, I wish I'd say no, but knowing me... But...mebbe this is Saint Des telling me to...to quit while I'm ahead." He bites his lip. "Thing is, my whole life, I thought I was a good guy, honest to God, I did. Someone who does the right thing, like you. Whenever I *didn't* do the right thing, there was always a good reason, an excuse, or each time I thought of it as a one-off.

"It was only when we did what we did to...to William Franklyn"—his voice shakes as he says the name, but he presses on—"that I realized I ain't that guy. I *never* do the right thing. I'm just a bad guy with de-lusions of goodness. But yesterday, Josh, *I did the right thing*, so right now, I *am* that guy I always wanted to be. So I...I *refuse* to regret it, 'least, not with my head.

Make sense?"

I grip his hand tightly with both my own. "Yeah," I whisper, 'cos there's a lump in my throat that's got nothing to do with being strangled and drowned yesterday. "Yeah, it does."

"Oh, and"—he grins, breaking the tension—"I am real glad you ain't dead, honest!" His face sobers again. "I deserve this. You don't. I mean...you wouldn't have gone near Jason's rex farm and riled him up so bad if I hadn't done what I'd done. And yesterday...well. This is totally *self-in-flic-ted*, as they say. Twice over."

I smile sadly 'cos there's some truth in that. We sit in silence for a while longer, but Wilhelm's looking stressed again, obviously dwelling on what's soon to happen.

"I wish they could do *something*," I mutter.

"They said sedation is a possibility," says Father Timaru. "But..."

"I said no," says Wilhelm. "Didn't wanna snooze the rest of my life away. Needed to talk to you. Anyway, feels like I've run away from practically everything my whole life long. I don't wanna run away from...from *this*. At least they said it'll be...be fairly quick when it...when it *happens*."

But he looks so scared. I fish out my rosary. "Shall we teach Father Timaru the Chaplet of Saint Desmond?" It's big with hunters, less so with city-folk.

He manages a weak smile. "Yeah, let's."

We go through the motions of teaching Father Timaru, though I suspect he knows it really and is just going along with us to help give Wilhelm a little more reason to concentrate, then Father Timaru teaches us the rosary in return. I've already learned it during confirmation prep, but I don't make that too obvious 'cos I don't want Wilhelm to feel thick.

Wilhelm dozes right off halfway through the Sorrowful Mysteries.

"He's just sleeping," says Father Timaru softly, with a glance at the steady heart monitor. *For now*, hangs in the air unsaid. Wilhelm must feel real bad, just from the concussion, even with the pain meds.

Quietly, we finish the Sorrowful Mysteries then move on to the Glorious ones. I sure don't wanna stop and think right now, 'cos my mind feels like a wasp's nest—if it gets a knock, it's gonna burst open and thoughts swarm out in all directions, total mad chaos.

We fall silent when we finish and mebbe that wakes Wilhelm, 'cos his eyes open.

"Hey, Bear."

He smiles—then memory spills into his eyes, and I can see the fear swamp him. His face screws up in terror, his throat working as he swallows.

I grip his hand tightly again. "Hey, you're probably gonna go straight to heaven, remember? That's real good. Nothing to worry about, huh?"

His nostrils flare and he takes several deep, shuddering breaths as he tries to getta hold of himself.

"I hope so," he whispers at last. "Y'know, I always figured if God was there, He were like my dad—all about punishment. Only worse, 'cos it would all be for stuff I'd *actually done*. But if He can forgive me like this…I guess He's *nice* instead. Nice as you."

"Nice as *me*?" I echo. "Bear, I'm *nice* like the sky over the prison on a cloudy summer night. God's nice like the sky out in the wilderness on the clearest winter midnight you can imagine."

The memory fills his eyes. "Beautiful," he whispers.

"Yep. Hey, Wilhelm?"

"Yeah?"

"When you see my dad and Uncle Z, can you tell them I love them and I'm trying to do what they want and live my life well, and I have people I love and who love me even if I can't be with them right now, and I'm okay?"

Wilhelm gets a real intent look and actually repeats the message back to me to check he's got it right.

"That's it, word perfect. Thanks, Bear. It makes me real happy to know they'll hear it from you." Never mind if they can hear me anyway, sending a personal message is special.

Wilhelm smiles, always so pleased to be told he's

got something right—but soon the fear creeps back. "Did I fall asleep during the praying?" he asks. "Was that bad?"

I squeeze his hand. "My dad used to say that if you fall asleep during a prayer, your guardian angel finishes it for you."

He relaxes a little. "That's real nice. But, uh, it was making me feel...um, I dunno...can we finish it?"

"Sure can. Here, take hold." I offer him my rosary beads.

He reaches for 'em then pauses, a scared look in his eyes.

"*Josh*..." His voice trembles, *scared* spilling into pure terror. "Josh, help me!" Pain chokes his words. I reach out, helplessly, and he lurches up, into my arms, clutching me like a little child. A very strong child. I wrap my arms around him and hold as tight as I can, rubbing his back, trying to soothe him.

"It's okay, Wilhelm," I whisper. "It's gonna be okay..."

He's breathing in tight, grunting groans, like he's in too much pain to speak, his face pressed to my neck. His heart pounds hard against my ribs, which he's probably gonna crack if he clings much harder, but that don't matter, all that matters is...

"It's gonna be okay, everything's gonna be okay. You're loved, Wilhelm. God loves you. I love you.

You're loved. It's gonna be okay…" I keep whispering it, over and over and over, until that big heart's stopped pounding against me and his arms have fallen away, and all of him's so limp and heavy, I'm afraid he's gonna slide right out of my grip onto the floor.

Desperately, I hold on. "Wilhelm?" I can't help whispering it, though I know…

Father Timaru's soft footsteps come around the bed; his hand touches my shoulder gently. "He's at rest now, Joshua, completely entrusted to God."

When I force my eyes open, the first thing I see is the silent heart monitor, showing a long flat line. Heck, he's so heavy, I really am gonna drop him…

"Here, Joshua, let me help you."

Father Timaru mostly supports Wilhelm's head as I manage to lay him back on the bed, stopping it flopping back in an undignified manner. For what it's worth. Death is terribly undignified. Wilhelm's mouth lolls open, his eyes staring blankly up at the ceiling.

…For a moment, I'm back in the 'Vi and Uncle Z's legs are buckling and he's falling and I'm clutching him and he's gasping, "Sorry, Josh, sorry," and he's not moving and he's staring up and his mouth's lolling and…

I break free of the memory. I'm starting to shake. I can't do nothing for Uncle Z now. Only Wilhelm…

I lift his muscle-heavy arms and cross them over his

chest, but then I just fold my arms over them and lay my head down on top and gasp and shake, 'cos I can't cry in-city like this with shackles on my legs, but it hurts *so much*.

Is there anyone I ain't gonna lose?

+

Eventually I manage to stop gasping for air like a dying fish and sit up again, my lungs and throat aching. And my ribs.

Heck, poor bear, I think you have *bruised me, but don't worry about it.*

Father Timaru gives my shoulder a squeeze. "I'm sorry. I know he was your friend."

He knows what Wilhelm told me, too, but that were confession so he ain't gonna say nothing about that to no one.

I sit in silence, thoughts cycling through my head.

Wilhelm was next-thing to a murderer.

Wilhelm was my friend.

Wilhelm is dead.

It all hurts so much.

+

Father Timaru moving in as though to close Wilhelm's sightless eyes snaps me out of it.

"Wait! We've gotta do it right."

"Right?"

"I need some cloth..." I hunt around in the bedside cabinet. The main cupboard is empty, but in the top drawer I find a small pile of candy wrappers and a single pigeon feather—the contents of Wilhelm's pockets, clearly. I also find a little stone with a *u* carved into it. He must've been waiting for a chance to slip it to me. Swallowing painfully, I put it in my own pocket.

But in the back of the drawer, I find a couple of lengths of bandage. Ideally, it should be a cloth woven specially, but that's fine for old folk dying at home in their camp. In other situations you use what's available.

Taking one of the pieces of bandage, I carefully weave knot-crosses into both ends, then shuffle to the sickly plant on the windowsill to collect the healthiest two leaves I can find and a good pinch of dirt. I put both ready on the bedside table then gather up half the dirt and try to wrap one pathetic leaf around it to make a little parcel.

Guess that's as good as it's gonna get. I open Wilhelm's mouth and slip it inside. "May your body rest in the soil from which it came and your soul unfurl in the presence of its Creator like a leaf in the sun," I recite.

Placing the cloth under Wilhelm's chin, I tie it tightly at the top of his head with an eternity knot to keep his mouth closed, then gather up the rest of the dirt, slide Wilhelm's left eye closed, and place the dirt on his lid. I take one of the bandage-end crosses and place it on top. "May the eyes of your body open to new life at the time of your Savior's choosing." I close Wilhelm's right eye and lay the leaf on top then place the second cross over it. "May the eyes of your spirit be open now in eternal life."

A second strip of bandage I wrap carefully around his eyes to hold everything in place, tying it with another eternity knot, and it's done. I didn't forget nothing. "Amen," I whisper.

"Amen," murmurs Father Timaru. "I have never seen that before. That's how hunters do it, is it?"

"Sure is," I whisper. "*Offering soil and leaf.*" Though since Wilhelm were city-born, he might not've actually cared all that much. I struggle to think. Soil and leaf is the priority, but... "Uh, he needs washing, next."

Father Timaru rests a hand on my shoulder for a moment. "That's not your job, Joshua, don't worry about it. There are people to do that."

"But it should be someone who cares. Who else..."

"I'm sorry, Joshua. I'm sure those two out there don't mind if you take a few minutes with him, but the morgue attendants will have to do everything like that."

"But that ain't right..."

"I'm sorry, Joshua."

Ugh, city-folk! They let strangers care for their dead? But if I make a fuss, they'll probably just drag me straight back to the prison.

I sink down in the chair again and sit with Wilhelm in silence until, finally, Father Timaru heads out of the room to notify the medical staff. Hurst soon looks in and says we'd better be going, so I lean forward to kiss Wilhelm's cooling brow.

"Poor frightened, tormented Bear," I whisper, "please be at peace."

But surely he is?

+

They put the hat down over my eyes again, but the drive passes in a blur. Am I going into overload? I don't take much in until I find the guards ushering me into Hunter One. The shackles are gone from my wrists and waist and ankles.

"Cub? Are you okay?" asks Ku.

I don't answer. The world spins erratically around me, out of control.

Hurst clears his throat uncomfortably. "Uh, I'm sorry to inform you that Fenn passed away about an hour ago at the hospital."

With a slight commiserating nod at them, he shoos Poulter out. The door clanks and clicks closed.

"Cub? Was it real awful?" asks Ku.

He clung to me like a frightened child... But the only thing they need to know is... "He saw the chaplain. He were right with God and Saint Des. He died well."

Billy snorts. "'Bout time that man did something well."

I spin around to face him. "He saved my life yesterday! I'd call that *doing something well*!"

"After *betraying* you, cub. He got what was coming to him."

"Billy, for once in your life, shut your pie-hole," snaps Ku, stepping quickly between us.

Yeah, my self-control is almost ragged enough to let me punch Billy right in his mean face—but I manage to turn my back on him, going to the window instead. I stare out, looking for birds, but there's none up there. I stare and stare, shaking more and more, until Ku wraps a blanket around me, and then his bony arms, rocking me gently from side to side.

"I know you can't cry right now, cub," he whispers. "But you can still get a hug."

+

At suppertime, I step out of the cell with Ku and Billy even though I don't feel hungry. My body probably is, and I shouldn't be alone.

"Where are Jason and Caleb?" I ask, the activity belatedly bringing me to myself enough to ask.

"Jason's in solitary," says Ku. "He'll get life, most likely, or something long enough that he won't be coming back here, anyways. Caleb was out on the balcony yesterday, probably keeping watch—supposed to distract or delay us if we came out, most likely. But he didn't actually do anything they'll be able to charge him with, so he's still here."

"We've kicked him outta the hunter pack, though," says Billy vindictively. "He can watch his own back. I 'spect he's having a fun time of it, by now. Though I'm guessing I'll be moving in with him soon as the Tazers notice he's on his own now." That comes out as a snarl.

"Sorry, Billy," I manage.

"*You* can't go in there and we butt heads more, so makes sense," he growls.

At the serving hatch, Dawn gives me an extra-large helping of bread and butter pudding. "I was terribly sorry to hear about Wilhelm Fenn," she says, her face drawn. "He always had a joke for everyone, and he did so love his desserts."

I muster an almost-smile and thank her, though I ain't sure I can eat it all.

Caleb's already at the hunter table, hunched up at the very far end where we never sit, all by himself. For a moment it takes me right back to when Seb left and Wilhelm was alone.

What's Caleb's life been like, dancing to Jason's tune? He ain't a nice guy—but having Jason for an older brother can't help no one.

As I get closer to the table I can see that he's got a black eye and a bruised chin, and he's trying to eat awkwardly with his good arm, like it hurts. And he ain't got no other hand, and that's partly 'cos of me.

"Looks like he's got some of his comeuppance already." Satisfaction fills Billy's voice.

I stop and stand still as tray-clutching orange-garbed figures swirl around me.

"Cub?"

I hurt so much; I just want all the suffering around me to *stop*.

"Cub? We gonna sit down?"

"Yeah." I head to the wrong end of the table and settle opposite Caleb. His head comes up, his eyes widening in disbelief.

"Have you gone stark mad, Raptor Boy?" snarls Billy, appearing at my shoulder.

"He's a hunter. He didn't actually fight with me, so he still gets protection."

"Protection? He woulda *stood* there while Jason—"

"Yeah?" I jerk to my feet, getting right in Billy's face for once, shaking with rage. "Well: *I. AIN'T. JASON.* Got that?"

I sit down again, quick, 'cos I'm one hair's breadth from totally losing it.

Frowning at Caleb, Ku settles beside me, resting a calming hand on my arm, reaching back with his other to do the same with Billy. "You sure about this, cub?"

When I nod, Billy thumps his tray down on the

other side of Ku and sits glaring across at Caleb like he wants to beat him up himself—and mebbe give me a good smack, too. But an air of disappointment ripples through the hall among those thugs who amuse themselves by picking on one-armed guys, at seeing their prey reabsorbed into a pack, even a real hostile one.

I start by eating my bread and butter pudding, in memory of Wilhelm, though I can't concentrate enough to taste it. My mind seethes.

We still don't know if William Franklyn is dead or alive, though it's sure looking bad. But at least we know who's responsible for it all. At least now we know where to look for answers.

I need to see Father Ben as soon as possible, get him on the case. By the time I'm released, in just weeks now, he can have gathered the information we need to plan our next step.

But how can we take that next step without me meeting Darryl and Harry and putting their custody plans at risk?

Guess we'll cross that bridge when we come to it. Father Ben first.

We've found out something at long last and I should feel ecstatic—but I can't. 'Cos right now it don't matter what Wilhelm told me, it don't matter what he did. I just want my friend to walk up to this table and put down his tray and sit beside me and crack some lame joke.

And he won't.

+

ACKNOWLEDGEMENTS

Being so different from the other books in the series and covering a larger timescale, A DIFFERENT KIND OF CAMOUFLAGE and A DIFFERENT KIND OF FREEDOM were tougher books to write. Despite working hard on them, there was still one thing about each that I was dissatisfied with when I finally gave up and sent them to my beta readers.

A big thank you to Marie C. Keiser and Antony Barone Kolenc for unerringly pinpointing those two problems—and helping me to fix them!

Thanks also to Theresa Linden for the inspiration for the blurb for A DIFFERENT KIND OF CAMOUFLAGE.

And many thanks to my other excellent readers and editors—Katy Huth Jones, Ruth P., Annette T., and Leslea Wahl—as well as all those who have helped with this series so far—and, of course, anyone I have forgotten!

Last but far from least, thanks to the Holy Spirit and to the two patron saints of the series, St. Francis of Assisi, who loved animals, and St. Ignatius of Loyola, who valued the imagination so highly.

You can make a difference!

Reviews and recommendations are vital to any author's success. If you liked this book, please write a short review—a few lines are enough—and tell your friends about the book too.
You will help the author to create new stories and allow others to share your enjoyment.

Your support is important. Thank you.

"Do they enjoy it?"

Fr. Jacob lifts his lined face and looks at me. Part of the reason I like him is that he doesn't insist on talking all the time. Often he just bows his head and prays for me. But I'm feeling unusually chatty today. Perhaps it's knowing this is almost the last time I'll see him.

"Who?" he asks.

"The victim witnesses."

"Ah." He purses his lips. "Some will tell you that they expect to. Most just talk about closure. That word comes up a lot. Unfortunately, I fail to see how watching a healthy human being with many decades of life ahead of them walk into a room under their own steam, only to be turned before their eyes into a lump of dead meat that needs wheeling out, can ever bring real healing to anyone."

Unbidden, a smile tugs at the corners of my mouth. "Don't you think it's rather insensitive of you to speak like that to me?"

Fr. Jacob shakes his head, blue eyes twinkling back at me, though mostly he looks very serious today. "To you, Carl? Are you bothered?"

I snort slightly and shake my head as well. "No. Not remotely."

Fr. Jacob sighs, the twinkle disappearing. He stares at me, and there's something on his face I haven't seen before. Despair?

"Cheer up," I tell him. "Plenty more inmates for you to talk into joining your club." That's why he's on edge today. He wants my soul for his God, and he hasn't got it. Baptism, that's what he wants me to want. "You're supposed to be retired, anyway."

He was already only a part-time chaplain when I arrived three years ago, and I'm the only one he's still visiting. This last year he's been getting frailer and frailer, and I'm pretty sure he's sick, really sick, but if I ask how he is, he just smiles, says, "As well as anyone almost four score can expect to be," and changes the subject. Clearly the two *of us are in a race as to who can meet our maker first. I'm fifty years younger, but it looks like I'm going to win, after all.*

"Other people have time," he's saying softly. "You haven't, and if anyone ever needed more time, it's you. I sometimes think that's what I hate most about this punishment. It takes away time and with it all hope of repentance."

I don't want to start all this again. Not today. "Repentance is for people who've done something wrong," I say harshly. "If there is a God—and you've far from convinced me—he'll see things my way."

"And if He doesn't?"

"I'm confident he will."

Fr. Jacob gives a really deep sigh this time. "Carl..." he sounds anguished. "Murder is a really grave sin. And you have committed it many times over. How can I make you understand before it is too late?"

"You can't, so stop wasting your breath. You're starting to sound like Pastor Garrett. You know Pastor Garrett?"

Fr. Jacob gives a crooked smile. "Yes, I know him."

"Well, he shows up once a month and shouts at me for an hour. Rants, waves his arms, strides up and down. Tells me I'm going to hell fifteen times for every one time he tells me God loves me. I've been counting. Not much else to do when he gets going. So don't you start telling me I'm evil filth too."

"Evil? No. I think of you more as a wounded child, alone and helpless in a dark wood. But don't think that lets you off the hook. God provided everything necessary for you to find your way out, and you ignored it all. So I am very afraid for you, my friend."

For the first time unease twists in my stomach. "Afraid for me?"

"Afraid for your soul."

I stare at him. He's never ranted at me. Never raved. Never preached hellfire and damnation. He's spoken about God's love and—when he understood that I don't believe love exists—he discussed rational proofs of God. It's all been quite interesting, intellectually speaking. Okay, he's told me how grave my sins are many times, but...with all his poor deluded talk of love, I've always assumed...

"Father..." There's an odd cold prickle down my spine. "Do you... Do you think I'm going to hell?"

He looks back at me, an odd expression on his face. "I cannot know where you are bound. I do not know what is in your heart, in your conscience, what is between you and God."

"I didn't ask you to say if I am; I asked you what you thought."

He's silent for a long, long while, this time. Finally I read the expression on his face: mingled horror and dismay. He must've thought I knew the answer to this question already. I keep silent, waiting.

"Well, if you do want my opinion," he says, when it's quite clear I really do, "You have murdered at least twelve people, in cold blood, for money. You have shown not the slightest remorse. The fact that you consider your own life just as unimportant as those of your victims shows consistency, but cannot excuse you. So yes, I very much fear you are going to hell, Carl Jarrold."

I blink in the evening light and lift my head. I've come close to dozing as I run over the memory of my last, disturbing, conversation with Fr. Jacob. The setting sun pours into the small cell they brought me to yesterday evening, after Fr. Jacob had gone. At least two guards are watching me at all times over the cameras. I suppose they expect me to rush to the window to watch the sunset, while thinking melancholy thoughts about it being the last one I'll ever see.

I almost snort out loud, at that. Why does everyone, from Fr. Jacob to the prison guards, find it so hard to believe that I really don't care? Why would I?

Love is the biggest lie out there. If people could see that, perhaps they'd understand. Human beings use one another and often when someone is useful to them they dress it up as "love." Fr. Jacob thinks he "loves" me, the poor lost sheep, but all he wants is another name to his account—though he doesn't realize it, poor deluded man. Everyone I've ever met has used me, from my mother onwards. Love doesn't exist. And Fr. Jacob is right about one thing. Without it, life is utterly meaningless. Why, then, should I care about losing life? Why should anyone? So how can killing someone be wrong?

That draws my thoughts back several weeks.

"Killing is *wrong, Carl."* Fr. Jacob sounded tired. Then again, he's always tired, now. "Can't you see that everyone but you believes that?"

"No, they don't. The State certainly doesn't or they wouldn't be going to do it to me. They can't have it both ways. It either is or it isn't. And clearly they believe it's fine, so long as it suits them. Typical human motivation, can't you see?"

Fr. Jacob rubs his forehead. "It is wrong to kill except in case of necessity. The fact that the State doesn't recognize that doesn't make it incorrect."

I shake my head at him pityingly. If I'd ever needed any confirmation of my beliefs, my death sentence has given it. Killing is no big deal, so long as it benefits the people doing it. So what did I do wrong? Nothing.

I open my eyes to the condemned man's cell again. I didn't have much in my own cell, but this place makes it look downright luxurious. Who cares? I like to be by myself. I like to be left to sit quietly and think. Death Row's been great for that. The less I have to do with people the better. Why are they even called people? Users. They're just users. Even Fr. Jacob, though I liked his visits. He's so oblivious to his deeper motivations. Actually believes what he's saying. It's charming, really. In a sad sort of way.

After he dropped his bombshell yesterday, an awkward silence fell. But soon Fr. Jacob turned to more practical matters.

"I've made arrangements for...for a proper burial."

"Really?" I'm surprised—but far from displeased. Since I've got no relatives, I was expecting to get cooked to ashes and stuck in the prison cemetery, but I've always preferred the idea of burial: natural recycling, after all. "But, uh, who's paying for it?" The State took all my money, not that Fr. Jacob would touch any of that wearing a full hazmat suit, double-gloved, and using tongs.

Fr. Jacob just smiles. "I've managed to acquire a plot in a local burial ground. Up by a wall."

"You make it sound so difficult. If it was too expensive, then forget it, seriously."

He smiles again. "No, not the money. I'm perfectly happy to part with that. But...well, it was rather hard to talk them into selling it to me. They were afraid they'd never be able to sell the adjacent one."

"Why not?" I ask blankly.

He just looks at me.

"Ah..." Yes, I'm one of the most reviled men in the country. I'm always forgetting that, since I don't feel I've done anything to deserve it. "How did you persuade them?"

Fr. Jacob laughs. "By buying the adjacent plot as well! That dealt with their objection, so they had to sell to me then."

"You bought two?" Discomfort stirs in my belly. That's a lot of money for a poor priest to spend, and I've still no intention of giving him what he wants. Baptism is about getting forgiveness for sins. I haven't done anything wrong, so I'm not doing it, even if it would make Fr. Jacob happy. "But what are you going to do with the second one?" It'll be a terrible waste, if it just lies there, empty and unused.

"Well, I can think of a perfectly appropriate use for it. It was time I made arrangements anyway."

I eye his pale skin—almost grayish today—and dark shadowed eyes. Just how sick is he? "You plan to be buried there?"

"Yes, Carl, I do. I'm sure you'll be relieved to hear it. I know how you feel about waste."

I stare at him. Before he told me I was going to hell, I wouldn't have been so surprised. Though I would also have been...surprisingly pleased. But now... "You're really happy to be buried near me? Even though I'm going to hell?"

A flicker of pain creases Fr. Jacob's brow. *"What I said...don't think I've given up on you, Carl."*

"But if I don't get baptized?" I challenge him. *"Because I'm not going to!"*

"Damnation isn't contagious, you know," he says gently. *"Especially once one is dead. But if you don't accept baptism...it doesn't change the fact that I care about you. That I consider you to be a friend. That I will not reject you as the rest of humanity has done. Even after death. Ultimately, only God will know your fate for certain."*

I look down at the floor, my throat oddly tight. "Well, in that case," I manage, *"thanks."*

The whole cell is orange now from the setting sun, but I stay put. I registered Fr. Jacob as my spiritual advisor seven days ago, so actually he could have been sitting here with me, for the whole of today. I didn't mind his daily visits this week, but after that last one yesterday...the thought of spending a whole day with him telling me I was going to hell, just the way Pastor Garrett does.

Well, I don't think he would have done, but every time he looked at me, I'd know what he was thinking. So I asked him not to come today. I felt bad, after him saying what he said about the burial, but considering what he'd told me earlier...what choice did I have?

"Are you sure?" The poor man sounded like he was in agony. *"Are you sure you don't want me to be here? I could just come to be in the witness gallery, later? Pop in to see you beforehand? In case you...change your mind?"*

Up until ten minutes ago, I might have said yes. But now I return a firm, "No. I will not change my mind, and you will not enjoy watching me die, so why should you go through that?"

"Carl..."

"I don't want you here. Don't come."

He looks at me for a while, in that sad way. "All right,"

he says at last. "It's your decision."

But as he's leaving he looks me straight in the eye and says, "Please, Carl, don't leave it too late." He closes his eyes and whispers, "Lord...please don't let him leave it too late."

His tone...utmost appeal...it makes my spine shudder. But he's spearing me with those blue eyes one last time, speaking with peculiar authority. "Don't leave it too late, Carl."

He clasps my hands, blesses me and leaves. And that's that.

**Get
THREE LAST THINGS
from your favorite retailer today!**

ABOUT THE AUTHOR

Corinna Turner has been writing since she was fourteen and likes strong protagonists with plenty of integrity. Although she spends as much time as possible writing, she cannot keep up with the flow of ideas, for which she offers thanks—and occasional grumbles!—to the Holy Spirit. She is the author of over twenty-five books, including the Carnegie Medal Nominated I Am Margaret series, and her work has been translated into four languages. She was awarded the St. Katherine Drexel award in 2022.

She is a Lay Dominican with an MA in English from Oxford University and lives in the UK. She is a member of a number of organizations, including the Society of Authors, the Catholic Writers Guild, Catholic Teen Books, Catholic Reads, the Angelic Warfare Confraternity, and the Sodality of the Blessed Sacrament. She used to have a Giant African Land Snail, Peter, with a 6½" long shell, but now makes do with a cactus and a campervan.

Get in touch with Corinna...

Facebook: Corinna Turner

Twitter: @CorinnaTAuthor

Don't forget to sign up for

NEWS
&
FREE SHORT STORIES
at:

www.UnSeenBooks.com

All Free/Exclusive content subject to availability.

www.ingramcontent.com/pod-product-compliance
Lightning Source LLC
Chambersburg PA
CBHW030754190726
48285CB00003B/856